PENGUIN SPECIALS

Penguin Specials fill a gap. Written by some of today's most exciting and insightful writers, they are short enough to be read in a single sitting – when you're stuck on a train; in your lunch hour; between dinner and bedtime. Specials can provide a thought-provoking opinion, a primer to bring you up to date, or a striking piece of fiction. They are concise, original and affordable.

To browse digital and print Penguin Specials titles, please refer to **www.penguin.com.au/penguinspecials**

ALSO BY SU TONG

Raise the Red Lantern: Three Novellas
Tattoo: Three Novellas
The Boat to Redemption
Binu and the Great Wall of China
Madwoman on the Bridge
My Life as Emperor
Rice

Petulia's Rouge Tin

SU TONG

Translated from the original Chinese by Jane Weizhen Pan and Martin Merz

PENGUIN BOOKS

UK | USA | Canada | Ireland | Australia
India | New Zealand | South Africa | China

Penguin Books is part of the Penguin Random House group of companies
whose addresses can be found at global.penguinrandomhouse.com.

This paperback edition was first published by Penguin Group (Australia), 2018

1 3 5 7 9 10 8 6 4 2

Text copyright © Su Tong, 1991

Translated from the Chinese by Jane Weizhen Pan and Martin Merz

Originally published in Chinese as *Hong Fen*
by Yuan Liou Publishing House, 1991

The moral right of the author has been asserted.

All rights reserved. Without limiting the rights under copyright reserved above, no part of this publication may be reproduced, stored in or introduced into a retrieval system, or transmitted, in any form or by any means (electronic, mechanical, photocopying, recording or otherwise), without the prior written permission of both the copyright owner and the above publisher of this book.

Cover design by Di Suo © Penguin Random House (Australia)
Text design by Steffan Leyshon-Jones © Penguin Random House (Australia)
Printed and bound in Hong Kong by Printing Express

ISBN: 9780734399496

penguin.com.au

Translators' Note

On the evening of 21 November 1949, over 2400 armed officers raided more than two hundred brothels in Peking in an operation that lasted all night. The brothels were closed and over a thousand women were rounded up.

Just over a month earlier, after the communist armies vanquished the Nationalist Government troops at the end of a bitterly fought civil war that followed the Second World War, the new socialist state of the People's Republic of China was inaugurated in the capital Peking, marking the birth of 'New China'.

The raids on brothels were part of a campaign launched by the Communist government to eliminate prostitution and 'reform prostitutes' in an effort to stamp out the vices of the 'Old Society' or Old China – which now referred to everything in China prior to 1949.

Similar raids were carried out in many other Chinese cities in the early 1950s, including Su Tong's hometown of Suzhou.

The women 'liberated' during this time were taken to enclosed facilities called Women's Labor Training Institutes. In reality, these institutes resembled prison camps where women were given medical examinations and treatment for venereal diseases as well as other health problems, educated in occupational skills and were forced to do manual labour and 'thought reform' sessions.

In the early 1960s, the government officially declared that it had eradicated STDs in mainland China.

Su Tong has commented that the past provides a clean canvas for him to work on. Inspired by a neighbour who was a former prostitute, Su Tong wrote this novella in 1991, some four decades after the events it describes. *Petulia's Rouge Tin* is one in a series of Su Tong's works with female protagonists including *Wives and Concubines*, which was adapted into the 1991 movie *Raise the Red Lantern*.

Although he did not witness the events of the early 1950s, Su Tong pays meticulous attention to the details of the time period to highlight the contrast of two worlds - high heels in the 'Old Society' versus humble slip-on shoes in the New China; a new set of politically correct vocabulary in the communist New China that confounded minds trapped in the past.

In the translation, we have tried to reproduce the effects of these particulars, although at times the significance of some details may be hard to identify for an English reader. We have inserted a minimum of intertextual explanations to assist the English reader as not to interrupt the flow of the narrative.

*

Chinese names in this translation are rendered in two ways:

Romanising into Wade-Giles

We made this decision to be consistent with the setting of the novel and to maintain the period mood.

The Wade-Giles system was developed in the nineteenth century and had been in common use in English language publications until 1979. The current Pinyin system was developed by the government of the People's Republic of China in the mid-1950s but was not widely adopted in publications in the West until the early 1980s.

Since the novel is set in China in the early 1950s, before the introduction of Pinyin, we feel that for this translation the Wade-Giles system is more time-appropriate than Pinyin. This is especially true as Su Tong tries to inject a nostalgic mood into his writing by using grammatical features of the traditional vernacular literary Chinese.

Translating the meaning of names

We feel the main female characters should not merely be transliterated. Qiu Yi/Chiu Yi and Xiao E/Hsiao E provide no hint about their roles. We have rendered their names as Autumn Grace and Petulia to capture something of the author's intent. Petulia was chosen because of its suggestive nature while also conveying the feel of the original Chinese name, which literally translates to a flower's calyx. Likewise, Lucky Phoenix is more revealing than a romanised rendition like Rui Feng.

*

Since the early 1920s, Chinese writers influenced by translated texts made extensive use of third person pronouns. Su Tong, however, mostly refers to characters by their names. He explains that he was trying to 'add some flavour of traditional vernacular literary Chinese.' While we are mindful of Su Tong's intention, this feature is hard to retain completely in the translation as it can make the English cumbersome and repetitive.

Western-style punctuation marks were officially introduced in Chinese in the early 1920s. Su Tong dispensed with quotation marks for dialogue in his novels in the 1990s. Instead, he opts to emulate traditional vernacular literary Chinese, which did not use quotation marks. We note that some writers and editors also remove quotation marks in English publications, which is considered unconventional in the English language. However, in this translation we do follow typographical conventions for clarity.

> Jane Weizhen Pan and Martin Merz
> 2017

Petulia's Rouge Tin

One morning in May, a truck from the army barracks stopped at the entrance of Emerald Cloud Lane. A bevy of gaudily attired prostitutes flaunting heavy makeup ambled out of the lane and clambered up over the truck's tailgate.

The onlookers that day included the street vendors usually stationed at the lane's entrance – the *shao-ping* baker, the cigarette vendor, the florist with the fragrant white champaca flowers that women pinned to their lapels – and a squad of young soldiers with rifles who stood ramrod straight like a row of trees on either side of the lane's entrance.

The last prostitutes to emerge were Autumn Grace and Petulia of Red Delight Pavilion. Autumn Grace was wearing a silk brocade Mandarin gown and high-heels. She leant against a doorframe as she bent over to smooth out her stockings below her knees. Petulia, who was following, looked as though she had just woken up; hair unkempt and dark circles under her eyes.

Autumn Grace led Petulia by the hand as they walked up to the wheat-bread stall.

'Miss Autumn, still want *shao-ping* today?' asked the baker.

'Of course,' said Autumn Grace. 'Why not?' She took two cakes and passed one to Petulia.

Petulia turned her head and looked at the girls already on the truck. 'I don't feel like eating,' she said. 'We have to go up there.'

Autumn Grace stood still, taking her time to rummage through her purse for change. She took a bite of the cake and chewed as she sauntered towards the truck. 'Why don't you want to eat?' she asked. 'Even condemned criminals are entitled to a hearty meal before they're executed.'

As they climbed on board, the truck's engine was already revving. Fifteen or sixteen prostitutes were assembled on the truck's bed, some sitting, others standing. Suitcases and bundles were piled up in one corner. Autumn Grace and Petulia stood by the railings of the truck bed and gazed up at the windows of Red Delight Pavilion. A pair of aquamarine panties dangling on a bamboo pole fluttered in the breeze.

'I forgot to take in the washing,' Petulia groaned. 'It might rain.'

'Don't worry about that,' said Autumn Grace. 'Who

knows if they'll even let us come back from wherever they're taking us.'

Dispirited, Petulia lowered her head. 'Why are they taking us away?'

'They said it was to check us for venereal diseases,' replied Autumn Grace. 'Let them. I'm sick of living. Even if they want to kill me I'm not afraid.'

The truck bounced along the narrow, potholed city streets, racing past all the familiar hotels, dance halls, opium dens, and gambling houses. The prostitutes appeared lost in their own thoughts; no one was tempted to offer an opinion on their fate. The truck's exhaust fumes quickly overpowered the perfume that had permeated the prostitutes' clothing.

In just a few days, red flags and slogans had blanketed the city, obscuring the old advertising posters featuring glamorous women. Children on the playground of a primary school across the street were practising gongs and drums for celebrations. A column of workers from the Ta-lung Machinery Factory marched towards the truck, singing revolutionary songs popular up north and waving coloured flags. Some pointed at the truck from Emerald Cloud Lane and sneered lewdly as it passed. One person broke away from the parade and spat at the women on the truck.

'Pigs!' the prostitutes shouted back. They crowded up to the railings and cursed at the spitter in unison, finally dissipating the sombre atmosphere on the truck. Suddenly, the truck sped up, leaving behind the crowd on the street. The women could tell the truck was heading towards the north of the city. At one point Autumn Grace spotted Mr P'u stepping out of a teashop and climbing onto a rickshaw.

She waved at him but he did not notice. 'Mr P'u, I'm leaving!' she cried out. Mr P'u did not hear her. Autumn Grace watched his lanky frame become smaller and smaller as the truck sped away. All she remembered was that Mr P'u wore a light grey suit and a fedora that day.

*

A temporary hospital had been set up in a Catholic church on the northern side of the city. Bullet holes were still visible all over the arched gate and the windows. Military doctors and nurses in white coats were rushing up and down the steps, and in and out of the church. 'Everyone from Emerald Cloud Lane, go upstairs!' an officer standing on the staircase commanded.

The prostitutes waited in line outside a curtained-off area. A woman inside called out their names.

'No hurry! Enter one by one!' she ordered.

'Who's in a hurry?' Autumn Grace taunted. 'It's not like we're queuing up to buy pig trotters.'

The prostitutes roared with laughter.

'Disgusting! This is just like pigs waiting to be castrated,' someone in the group added.

The officer who had escorted them in pointed his gun at the speaker. 'Shut up!' he yelled. 'This is for your own good!' His expression was so stern the prostitutes immediately fell silent. One of them, called Lucky Phoenix, became deeply absorbed in biting her fingernails and spitting the parings onto the floor.

Soon Petulia's name was called, but she stood frozen, as if in a trance. Autumn Grace prodded her. 'They called your name!'

Petulia clung to Autumn Grace's arm. 'I'm scared. Please, let's go in together,' she pleaded.

'What are you afraid of?' said Autumn Grace. 'You don't have the pox. Let them check. You only have to take your clothes off.'

Petulia's lips trembled, as if she were about to burst into tears.

'You're so useless,' fumed Autumn Grace, stamping her foot. 'Alright, I'll go in with you.'

On the other side of the curtain, Petulia curled up on a bed. Since childhood she had been afraid of doctors and the smell of ethanol. The female army doctor's face was hidden behind a surgical mask, revealing only a pair of cold, thin-slitted eyes.

She waited for Petulia to undress but Petulia held her hands firmly against her underwear.

'I'm not sick,' she bleated. 'I don't want to be examined.'

'Everyone has to be examined, regardless of whether they are sick or not,' the doctor retorted.

'It's that time of the month. I can't do it.'

The doctor knitted her brow, clearly annoyed. 'You really are being difficult,' she said, menacingly extending her latex-gloved hand.

At that moment Petulia heard the sound of someone passing wind. When she looked over, Autumn Grace winked at her.

'Loathsome!' the doctor shrieked.

'You mean we can't even fart?' said Autumn Grace, rolling over. 'Who will be responsible if I explode?'

Petulia covered her mouth to hide her giggling. The women waiting on the other side of the curtain laughed in concert.

'Stop it!' the young officer barked at them. 'This is not a whorehouse.'

Several girls from other establishments had been determined to have venereal diseases. They were instructed to sit on a long bench to await their fate. Some of them were weeping.

The other prostitutes began to file down the church steps.

Autumn Grace and Petulia walked arm in arm. Petulia looked deathly pale. She surveyed the dilapidated church and took out her handkerchief to wipe her brow. Then she wiped her neck, her arms and her legs. 'I feel filthy,' she whimpered.

'You know what? I farted deliberately,' Autumn Grace announced. 'I held back just for that.'

'What will happen to us?' asked Petulia. 'Do you know where they'll take us next?'

'Who knows.' Autumn Grace sighed. 'I heard they will make us do hard labour. I'm not afraid of that, but I am worried you won't be able to cope.'

'I'm not afraid of hard labour,' replied Petulia, shaking her head. 'I just don't know how I'll get by in the future. I'm scared.'

The green army truck was still parked at the gate of the temporary hospital. Most of the girls had climbed back up onto the truck bed. Autumn Grace's expression suddenly turned dismal as they neared the gate.

'We're done for! They're not going to let us go back to Emerald Cloud Lane,' she said in a hushed voice.

'What should we do? I haven't packed.' Petulia moaned.

'Let's find a place to hide for now, and see,' whispered Autumn Grace.

Autumn Grace then led Petulia by the hand and the two of them hid behind a nearby wooden shed. The soldiers obviously used the spot to relieve themselves. The stench was so confronting the women quickly covered their noses. They did not notice a young soldier squatting in the grass. He was about eighteen or nineteen years old and had a round and ruddy face. Holding his trousers with one hand, he brandished his rifle with the other and pointed it at the two women. Petulia screamed. They had to head back.

'Hurry up, you two! Get on the truck!' the officer yelled. 'Now!'

Autumn Grace and Petulia climbed up onto the truck. Autumn Grace whined non-stop at the officer. 'Are you going to kill us? At least tell us if you are! Why keep us in the dark? Where are you taking us?'

The officer was unmoved. 'Shut up!' he said. 'We have orders to take you to the Women's Labour Training Institute.'

'But I didn't bring anything with me!' cried Autumn Grace, stomping her feet. 'Not a penny! Not even a pair of spare panties. What do you want me to do?'

'You don't need to bring anything. You will all be issued daily necessities when you get there,' said the officer tersely.

'Who cares about *your* things! I want my own belongings – my jewellery, my silk Mandarin gowns, my stockings. And what about my sanitary belt? Will you issue me that?' Autumn Grace snapped.

The officer's face darkened. 'You're being recalcitrant! I'll shoot you if you don't shut up!'

Petulia squeezed Autumn Grace's hand. 'Please, please. I beg you. Don't say anything more.'

'I don't believe he'd dare to shoot,' countered Autumn Grace.

Petulia started to sob. 'We've ended up here, so what's the point of keeping those things? Either way, we're doomed. Why bother?'

The North Gate came into view in the distance. The red flags on the city wall were fluttering in the midday breeze. The women on the truck realised they were about to be tossed out of the prosperous city they were so familiar with. Some of them began to wail.

'Officer, please! Let us go back,' they pleaded. But the young officer stood bolt upright, stony-faced. The women near him could sense his accelerated breathing and a heavy garlic odour.

The truck slowed down as it passed through the North Gate. Autumn Grace's palms became cold and clammy. She squeezed Petulia's fingers once and then suddenly jumped off the truck.

Petulia saw Autumn Grace's body glance off the brick wall of the city gate and then bounce to the ground. Her friend's escape happened very fast and triggered a wave of screeching from the women on the back of the truck.

Petulia was momentarily stunned. She grabbed the officer's hand and pleaded, 'Don't shoot! Please! Let her go!' and then turned back to watch her friend.

Autumn Grace jumped up from the ground, kicked off her high heels and dashed away, one hand holding up the hem of her gown. She ran fast and disappeared through the city gate in a flash.

The young officer fired a warning shot into the air. Petulia heard him blurt a revolting curse in his Shantung provincial patois, 'Damned stinkin' whore!'

*

In late spring of 1950, Petulia arrived at the Women's Labour Training Institute, a labour camp located in a remote valley. This was only the second place she had lived since leaving her birthplace, the township of Hengshan. The Institute consisted of rows of single storied structures with white walls and red-tiled roofs. A few peach trees near the buildings were in blossom, their pink flowers emitting a hint of warming comfort. Standing in front of the peach trees, Petulia finally stopped weeping.

The Institute was nestled in amongst meandering hills with only a dirt road to the outside world. There was no barbed wire perimeter fence, but at the entrance stood a tall watchtower with a guard monitoring activities in the camp.

Upon arrival, Lucky Phoenix told the others that she had been to this place before, when it was a Japanese army barracks.

'What were you doing here?' asked Petulia.

'Sleeping with Japanese soldiers, of course. What else could I be doing,' said Lucky Phoenix, biting her fingernails.

There were no beds inside the dormitory. Instead, were several brick platforms for communal sleeping. Six women shared each platform. The officer told the prostitutes to choose a place for themselves.

'Let's sleep next to each other,' Lucky Phoenix said to Petulia.

Petulia sat quietly on the brick platform staring at the stains on the mud wall and the spiderwebs. She thought about Autumn Grace and wondered where she had gone. Petulia would have felt better if Autumn Grace was still with her. Over the years, Autumn Grace had become the mainstay of her life – she had relied on Autumn Grace for everything. Now Petulia felt even more anxious without Autumn Grace.

None of the prostitutes could sleep on the first night in the Women's Labour Training Institute. The brick platforms were infested with fleas and bedbugs. Rats constantly leapt onto the prostitutes' faces from their nests in the gaps between the walls. Screaming and cursing reverberated in the room all night.

'How can this damn place be fit for human habitation!' Lucky Phoenix grumbled.

'No one wants to treat you like a human, anyway.

You're lucky you haven't been shot dead!' someone else snapped in the darkness.

'What do they want us to do here?' asked Lucky Phoenix. 'Sleep with men?'

The other prostitutes laughed and did not hide their disdain for her absurd question.

'I can't sleep,' a prostitute shouted at a patrolling guard in the middle of the night 'Give me a sleeping pill.'

The guard stood impassively in the distance. 'Carry on as much as you want! Tomorrow you will learn what hard labour means,' he bellowed. 'You think you are here to be pampered? No! You are here to be thoroughly reformed through labour! Can't sleep? Then don't!'

'What does 'reform' mean?' Lucky Phoenix asked Petulia.

'I don't know,' said Petulia, shaking her head, 'and I don't want to know.'

'What does it mean? It means they won't let you sell yourself anymore!' another prostitute giggled. 'They will force you to do hard labour to forget about men. Then you will never dare to seduce a man again.'

Petulia finally dozed off shortly before dawn. She had one nightmare after another. Then she was woken up by the sound of the other prostitutes taking turns to urinate into a bucket.

She felt exhausted, as if she were about to fall apart. She sat up and leaned against the wall, then turned her head to look outside. A branch of a peach tree was just outside the window. Dewdrops were settling on the delicate peach blossoms. Just as Petulia was about to pick a sprig, reveille sounded from the watchtower. She shivered. Suddenly she realised her life in an unfamiliar world had begun.

*

It was already pitch-dark by the time Autumn Grace made it back to Red Delight Pavilion. The lanterns that used to adorn the entrance were gone. Autumn Grace hastily primped her hair in the dark. The gate was tightly shut but she could hear the faint sound of mahjong tiles being shuffled. She knocked on the door for a long time. Finally, the madam of Red Delight Pavilion opened the door.

'Why did they let you go?' she asked in disbelief.

Autumn Grace barged in without responding. 'Did you run away?' the madam asked as she followed her. 'We'll be in trouble if you did. They will come back for you tomorrow for sure. Things are very tense these days.'

'What are you afraid of, if I'm not afraid?' Autumn Grace snapped. 'I'm just here to get my things.'

'What things?' the madam asked. 'The soldiers confiscated your jewellery and valuables.'

Autumn Grace bounded up the stairs. 'Don't try to

pull a fast one on me,' she yelled. 'You should be more worried that god will strike you down with a bolt of lightning for swiping my things.'

Autumn Grace's room was a mess. Sure enough, her jewellery box had disappeared. She rushed back downstairs and shouted at the four mahjong players. 'So, my jewellery has become your mahjong chips?'

'Autumn Grace, you are not being fair,' said the madam as she picked up another mahjong tile. 'I always treated you like my own daughter for all those years. How could you possibly think I embezzled your hard-earned money?'

A contemptuous smile appeared on Autumn Grace's face.

'You once relied on me to bring in money. Now things have changed. As the saying goes: the tree falls and monkeys disperse. You think I don't know you?'

The madam's face darkened. 'Help yourself and look for your things if you don't believe me! I don't have the patience to argue with you!' she riposted.

'I don't have the patience either,' Autumn Grace shot back. 'But I'm not someone who can be bullied easily. And I'm capable of anything.'

'What would *you* dare to do?' the madam shrilled.

Autumn Grace circled the mahjong table with her arms folded.

'Well, the easiest thing would be to set this place

alight so I won't have to look at your stinkin' whorehouse ever again.'

The madam snorted. 'You don't have the guts to do it. You should be more worried that I'll get someone to gouge out your little cunt and feed it to dogs.'

'Me? Afraid? I have never been afraid of anything since I fell in with you and your stinking whorehouse at sixteen. What's the big deal about gouging out my cunt? I wouldn't blink even if my heart were gouged out!' Autumn Grace snarled.

Then she dashed down the stairs, ripped a painting from the wall and rammed the paper into the stove to start a fire. The mahjong players rushed to restrain her.

'Burn! Burn!' screamed Autumn Grace brandishing the flaming painting. 'I'm burning this whorehouse down! No one gets out alive!'

'Autumn Grace! Are you mad?' someone asked.

'Yes, I am mad!' Autumn Grace yelled. 'I've been mad since I ended up here at the age of sixteen!'

In the midst of this chaos downstairs, the madam tossed a small cloth-wrapped bundle from the top of the staircase. 'Everything is there. Take it and get lost. Now!'

Autumn Grace walked out of Emerald Cloud Lane carrying the small cloth-wrapped bundle. It was late at night. Standing on the deserted street, she suddenly was overwhelmed by a wave of dejection. She turned around to look at the Red Delight Pavilion and saw

Petulia's aquamarine panties still fluttering under the evening sky. Emerald Cloud Lane was still where it had always been but in just a few days, the whole world had changed and all the girls in the lane had been driven out permanently. Autumn Grace was concerned about Petulia but she had more than enough problems of her own to worry about.

In the dim streetlight, Autumn Grace found her bearings. She decided to head to the northern sector of the city to seek out Mr P'u. After all, Mr P'u ought to be her first port of call.

*

Mr P'u lived in the unmarried quarters of the electric company's dormitory block. When Autumn Grace arrived, the night watchman had just opened the building's iron gate. 'Mr P'u is not in,' the watchman told Autumn Grace. 'He's often away overnight.'

'That's alright,' said Autumn Grace. 'I'll wait for him upstairs.'

Autumn Grace was certain that she knew Mr P'u's habits better than the watchman did. She stood outside Mr P'u's room patiently waiting for him to return. Unmarried male employees of the electric company, carrying towels and mugs, entered the communal bathroom. One, standing by the sink, turned to study

Autumn Grace's face. 'Looks like she's from Emerald Cloud Lane,' he conjectured. Autumn Grace pretended not to hear. She retrieved a cigarette and smoked unhurriedly as she speculated about where Mr P'u might have gone. *Perhaps he went to a teahouse for breakfast, or perhaps linked up with a girl from another brothel. He is, after all, a master of self-indulgence.*

'Why are you here?' Just as Autumn Grace was becoming anxious, Mr P'u returned. He opened the door with his key, grabbed her with his other hand and ushered her into his room.

'I had nowhere else to go,' explained Autumn Grace as she sat on a sofa. 'The People's Liberation Army sealed off Emerald Cloud Lane. All the girls were loaded onto a truck and taken away to who knows where. I jumped off the truck and escaped.'

'So I heard.' Mr P'u frowned and stared at Autumn Grace. 'And what do you plan to do now?'

'Heaven only knows. It's very tense everywhere right now. They're arresting people and forcing them to do hard labour. I'm not doing hard labour. I'll hide out here for a while. Mr P'u, surely you and I are close enough for you to let me stay here.'

'Not a problem. Of course, I will help you,' said Mr P'u as he sat Autumn Grace on his lap to embrace her. 'However,' he continued, 'there are too many prying eyes here. I think it best to take you to my family home and let it be known that you are our new maid.'

'Why are you being so mean?' she pouted. 'Why not just say I'm your new wife?' Autumn Grace wrapped her arms around Mr P'u's neck and kissed him, then playfully thumped him on the back with her fist.

'Alright. Whatever you want.' Mr P'u gently lifted her gown to peek inside. 'Autumn Grace,' he sighed. 'You'll be the death of me. You've always beguiled me.'

Autumn Grace pretended to spit on the ground. 'Sweet talk means nothing to me,' she retorted. 'I really would like to gouge a man's heart out with a knife to look closely and see what it's made of. Probably just filthy mud. Then I would no longer harbour any illusions.'

The two of them dined on wonton soup and a steamer of miniature pork buns at a Wu-hsi cuisine wanton shop. Then they hailed a rickshaw on the street. 'Now I will take you to my family home,' Mr P'u announced. Autumn Grace covered part of her face with a silk scarf and held Mr P'u's arm as the rickshaw threaded its way through the bleak and disorderly streets. Cinemas were still showing Hollywood movies; the heroes and beautiful women on the movie billboards were as enamoured with each other as ever. Autumn Grace pointed to a billboard. 'You see that couple,' she said. 'They're fake.'

'What's fake?' asked Mr P'u, puzzled.

'It's all fake,' said Autumn Grace. 'Your kindness to me is fake. My ardour for you is fake. Sealing off Emerald

Cloud Lane is fake, too. I just can't believe that men don't like to visit brothels. Is this world any purer for throwing us out?'

The rickshaw lurched as it entered a secluded street. 'That's my home,' said Mr P'u, pointing to a small yellow structure. 'My father bought it before he died. Now my mother lives there with a maidservant. There are plenty of empty rooms.'

Autumn Grace jumped down from the rickshaw. 'How should I address your mother?'

'Call her Mrs P'u.'

'Alright,' said Autumn Grace. 'I'm not good at dealing with women. Does she know my background? If your mother was in the same profession as me it would be so much easier for us to get on with each other.'

'Don't talk nonsense!' scolded Mr P'u. 'My mother comes from a good family, so you'd better behave in front of her. Best to say you're a colleague of mine. Don't you dare let the cat out of the bag.'

Autumn Grace giggled. 'That's a tall order. I'm not good at faking things.'

Mrs P'u was sitting on a rattan chair knitting. Autumn Grace became a little timid as soon as she saw Mrs P'u's large bright eyes. *Women with piercing eyes like that are usually difficult to deal with*, she thought. The greetings were simple yet uneasy, and Autumn Grace's eyes flitted about absent-mindedly. All the while she felt Mrs

P'u's eyes poking and prodding her body from top to toe, sizing her up. She also found Mrs P'u's regional accent grating.

The maid led Autumn Grace to a room upstairs that obviously had been unoccupied for a long time, judging from the layers of accumulated dust.

'Miss,' said the maid, 'please rest in the living room. I'll clean this up in no time.'

Autumn Grace waved her hand. 'You may leave. I'll clean it up myself.'

Autumn Grace opened a window and looked down into the garden. Mr P'u and his mother were standing in the garden in conversation. Autumn Grace heard Mrs P'u suddenly raise her voice.

'Don't lie to me,' scolded Mrs P'u. 'I could tell what kind of garbage she is as soon as I set eyes on her. People will laugh at you. Don't you care?'

Autumn Grace knew she was expected to hear what had just been said. She didn't care. Since childhood, she never cared what other people said – whatever was said about her simply meant nothing to her.

*

Every day from morning till dusk Petulia had to sew thirty hessian sacks. Like everyone else she had an assigned task and was not allowed to stop before her quota was fulfilled. The young women were crowded together in an old munitions warehouse sewing hessian sacks. Their days became long and tedious. The sacks were for the military, and every day a truck would arrive to transport the sacks out of the camp.

Petulia's slender fingers became covered with blood blisters and eventually, she was unable to hold the needle. Confronted by a stack of hessian sheets she wept. 'I can't finish sewing,' she moaned. 'My fingers are about to fall off.'

'In a few days you'll get better at it,' said the women nearby. 'The blisters will drain and calluses will form, and then you'll be fine.'

Eventually, everyone in the room finished their task and left, except Petulia, who was still surrounded by unfinished hessian sacks. When it became dark, Petulia heard the soldier outside the door pacing back and forth. 'Number 8, haven't you finished?' he yelled impatiently. 'You fall behind every day!' Petulia sat stiff as a board on a pile of hessian sacks. *I don't want to sew anymore. They can do whatever they want with me.*

The old munitions warehouse was filled with the bitter, grassy scent of hemp. It was becoming darker outside. *Click.* The soldier turned on the light. 'Number 8, why are you just sitting there? You wanna be locked up in solitary confinement?' he shouted.

Petulia slowly raised her hands to show her fingers.

She had wanted to explain but did not bother to utter a word. The soldier walked away grumbling. Then Petulia heard him singing a popular revolutionary song:

The sky in the liberated zone is always blue and bright,
The people in the liberated zone are always happy and light

About half an hour later, the soldier on duty walked into the old munitions warehouse and saw Petulia tying a rope on a beam, feebly positioning her head in the noose and tightening it with one hand. The soldier panicked. 'Number 8! Freeze!' he barked and fired a warning shot.

Petulia turned around to look at the soldier while holding the noose around her neck. 'Why did you shoot?' she asked. 'I'm not going anywhere.' The soldier pointed at the rope and asked, 'You want to die?' Petulia nodded apathetically. 'Yes, I want to die. I can't finish sewing the thirty sacks. What do you want me to do?'

After the shot rang out, people ran towards the old munitions warehouse. Some of the prostitutes craned forward to peer through the window. 'Petulia, did he shoot you?' asked Lucky Phoenix.

A young officer and a few soldiers escorted a staggering Petulia out of the warehouse. 'I can't finish sewing thirty sacks! I have no choice but to die,' lamented Petulia, covering her face with her handkerchief.

Then the prostitutes started to wail in unison. 'Stop crying!' the officer bellowed. 'Whoever doesn't stop will be shot dead!'

'We are not allowed to kill ourselves, and even crying is forbidden. How are we supposed to live?' someone in the crowd protested. 'Why don't you shoot us all and be done with it!'

A gaggle of prostitutes then rushed up to grab the legs of the officer and the soldiers. They tore off their uniforms and squeezed their genitals. In an instant, the labour camp descended into chaos. The searchlight on the watchtower zeroed in on the scene and gunshots reverberated. Petulia jumped behind a wall to take refuge, dumbfounded by the battle she had precipitated. She never imagined it would result in this.

Reports of the prostitutes' disturbance at the Women's Labour Training Institute even made it into the newspapers. That was in late spring of 1950. As news reports are always concise they did not mention Petulia's name, let alone that she was the catalyst.

*

The next morning Petulia was summoned to the administrative office at the Training Institute. There were several female cadres in charge of women's work, all with identical short haircuts. Their expressions were odd as they sized her up. Then they conferred in whispers amongst themselves before commencing an excruciatingly long 'conversation.'

Petulia had not slept well, and when she realised that she had precipitated a catastrophe she was breathless with fear. *It wouldn't be so bad if they simply shot me, but what if they increase my quota to forty or even fifty hessian sacks? I'll just have to find another way to die. If only Autumn Grace were here; she'd help me. But Autumn Grace abandoned me and ran away.*

The 'conversation' with the female cadres lasted the whole morning. Petulia was absent-minded, her head lowered as she stared at her feet the whole time. She noticed a hole in the silk stocking she had worn all the way from Emerald Cloud Lane, through which poked out a deathly pale swollen toe.

'Petulia, please tell us about your experiences,' said one woman cadre smiling solicitously. 'Don't be afraid. We're all class sisters.'

Petulia shook her head weakly. 'I don't want to talk about it,' she said. 'I can't finish sewing thirty sacks. That's all. I have nothing more to say.'

'Your attitude is not conducive to becoming a reformed person,' said the woman cadre calmly. 'Tell us why you wanted to die. Tell us about your suffering, we are all class sisters. We also suffered in the Old Society.'

'I already told you. I have blisters on my fingers and can't sew thirty sacks, so I might as well die.'

'That is not the main reason. The brothel exploited and oppressed you for many years. You suffered bitterly in the Old Society and are consumed by a deep-rooted class hatred. Yet you were powerless to resist. Yesterday you were afraid you would fall into the clutches of your enemies again, so you wanted to die. Am I right?'

'I don't know.' Petulia kept her head lowered and stared at the hole in her stocking. 'I'm scared.'

'Don't be afraid. No one can hurt you now. You were brought here to reform yourself and give you a chance to be a new person in the New Society as soon as possible. Brothels are products of the Old Society, and they have been eliminated. What do you want to do in future? Be a worker? Or perhaps a shop clerk?'

'I don't know. I'm happy to do anything as long as it's not too tiring.'

'Good. Now, Petulia, tell us about how you fell into the clutches of the madam at the brothel. We want to help you. We want you to attend the women's meeting next month to denounce the madam and the brothel owner for exploitation and oppression.'

'I don't want to,' said Petulia. 'How can you talk about such things in public? I wouldn't be able to say anything.'

'We are not asking you to talk about *those* filthy things,' the woman cadre said, blushing slightly. 'It's a denunciation. Do you understand? For example, you can denounce the way the brothel tricked you into their trap and how they beat you up when you attempted to escape. It's all right if you exaggerate a little. The important thing is to reclaim a debt of blood from your enemies. After that all you have to do is shout a few slogans.'

'I can't do a denunciation, I really can't,' said Petulia indifferently. 'Perhaps you don't know that I signed a contract to prostitute myself at Red Delight Pavilion. Besides, they never beat me up. I took in customers to earn an honest living. Why would they want to beat me?'

'You are saying you entered Red Delight Pavilion on your own volition?'

'Yes.' Petulia lowered her head again. 'I was sixteen when my father died and then my mother remarried. I had to leave my hometown and come here to work. No one looked after me. I had to earn money to look after myself.'

'Why didn't you work in a silk reeling factory? We were born poor, too, but we all worked silk reeling factories. We earned enough money to live on.'

'*You* don't mind slaving away in a factory, but I can't take it.' Petulia appeared completely inconsolable. She covered her face with her hands and whimpered. 'All of you are from good families. But I was born a whore. I have no choice, I was born a whore.'

The female cadres were at a loss for words. After

directing a few more comments at Petulia they departed. Then the officers in military uniform entered. One tossed a small bundle to her feet and said, 'Number 8, your older sister sent you some things.'

As soon as Petulia saw the scarf tied around the bundle she knew Autumn Grace had asked someone to deliver it to her. Inside the bundle were silk stockings, bars of soap, toilet paper and snacks. Petulia realised that Autumn Grace had not forgotten about her and that in this ever-changing world, the bond between her and Autumn Grace was everlasting.

Petulia unwrapped a piece of toffee and put it in her mouth. The toffee somewhat restored Petulia's faith in life. Her waist swayed as usual when she walked past the soldier's quarters while chewing the toffee. Petulia was a slender girl with a willowy waist. She unwrapped another piece in front of the old munitions warehouse. She spotted a soldier on duty standing under a peach tree. 'Sir, would you like a toffee?' asked Petulia with a seductive smile. The soldier knitted his eyebrows and turned away. 'Who would touch your toffee? Disgusting!'

*

It was Mr P'u who had delivered the bundle to the Training Institute. Initially, he did not want to go, but he finally succumbed to Autumn Grace's badgering.

'Mr P'u, this will prove if you have any decency,' said Autumn Grace.

'Which Petulia is it? You don't mean the scrawny little waif?'

'You may be fond of voluptuous women, but others prefer slight physiques. No need to be so snide. She often praised you as a suave gentleman, so aren't you the bastard?'

Autumn Grace did not dare go outdoors. Sleeping became her principal activity to while away the time. She slept alone during the day and accompanied Mr P'u at night. In an instant, her months and years in Red Delight Pavilion floated away. Now her status was uncertain. She envisaged that in future she might still need to depend upon a man, though it was possible that all she could rely upon was the small bundle of jewellery that she had accumulated over the years. Autumn Grace sat on the bed and spread out her collection of rings and bracelets. She began to estimate the value of each piece. The gold jewellery would be enough to live on for five or six years. That gave her comfort.

One bracelet that Autumn Grace liked the most was engraved with a dragon and phoenix design. She slid it onto her wrist then suddenly thought of Petulia who once had a similar dragon-phoenix bracelet. Now Petulia had nothing. Autumn Grace could not imagine what Petulia's life would be like in the future. *The moment a woman has no money she can only depend on a man, but men are never reliable.*

Half a month passed in a flash. Autumn Grace felt Mrs P'u's attitude towards her rapidly deteriorate. One day over lunch, Mrs P'u got straight to the point: 'When are you leaving?'

'What? Are you evicting your guest?'

'You are not a guest,' Mrs P'u sneered. 'I never invited you into my home. Letting you stay for half a month is giving you more than enough face.'

'No need for that attitude,' said Autumn Grace calmly. 'You don't scare me. Whatever you have to say, say it to your son. If he tells me to leave, I'll leave.'

'I have never in my life encountered such a despicable wench,' said Mrs P'u, slamming down her chopsticks. 'Do you think I'm afraid to tell him?'

That day when Mr P'u returned home, Mrs P'u intercepted him in the garden. Autumn Grace heard Mrs P'u wailing as she harangued her son for a very long time. Autumn Grace found her behaviour laughable, though she did feel some pity for Mrs P'u, too. *But why all the drama?* Autumn Grace was not planning to malinger in the P'u residence for long. She just did not like her stay ending in expulsion. That was too great a loss of face.

Mr P'u appeared terribly embarrassed when he came upstairs. Autumn Grace smiled as she looked into his eyes, waiting for him to speak. She wanted to see how

Mr P'u would handle the situation. He went straight to the bathroom to take a shower.

'Would you like me to scrub your back?' asked Autumn Grace.

'No,' replied Mr P'u. 'I can do it myself.'

She heard water splashing, and then Mr P'u's muffled voice: 'Autumn Grace, tomorrow I'll find you another place to live.'

Autumn Grace was momentarily stunned. Then she kicked open the bathroom door. 'You really are useless,' she shrieked, gesticulating at Mr P'u. 'I was blind to have trusted you.'

Mr P'u put his mouth over the faucet, then spat out some water. 'I have no choice,' he said. 'Anyway, a move would be good. It will be more convenient for us to be together.'

Autumn Grace said nothing more. She stuffed her possessions as quickly as she could into a leather case she had recently bought. Then she stood in front of the dresser, looking into the mirror as she combed her hair and lightly applied makeup.

Mr P'u came out of the bathroom with a towel wrapped around his waist. 'You're leaving?' he asked. 'Where will you go?'

'None of your business,' she snapped. 'Now give me the money.'

'What money?' asked Mr P'u, puzzled.

Autumn Grace hurled her wooden comb at him. 'What do you think? I've been sleeping with you every night, do you expect me to whore for free?'

Mr P'u picked up the wooden comb and put it on the dresser. 'Don't be silly, we're just moving. Why are you being grumpy?'

Autumn Grace, still fuming, kicked Mr P'u. 'Quick! Give me the money. This is the last time I'll take a customer, and this last customer was a dog.'

Mr P'u retrieved some money from his wallet, mumbling, 'How much do you want? I'll give you whatever you ask for.'

Autumn Grace burst into tears. She snatched the banknotes, tore them up, then hurled the scraps at Mr P'u's face. 'Who wants your money? Mr P'u, have I ever asked for money from you? You heartless bastard!' she shouted.

After evading Autumn Grace's attack, Mr P'u sank into the sofa, panting. 'Then what *do* you want?' he asked. 'You may stay for a few more days if you don't want to leave.'

Autumn Grace, suitcase in hand, shrieked, 'Go to hell!' then ran down the stairs. She bumped into Mrs P'u in the garden, who gloated upon seeing the suitcase. She spat at Mrs P'u and shouted, 'You hypocritical witch, I'll be praying you die a miserable death.'

*

Autumn Grace initially wanted to return to her family home. The rickshaw arrived at the slum where she grew up. Children were running around and chasing each other on the unpaved street. Newly washed clothes and nappies, still dripping, hung from bamboo poles over the street. The familiar sour stench of filth and poverty pervaded the air.

Autumn Grace then saw her old blind father sitting in the doorway stringing broad beans, while her aunt, sleeves rolled up, ladled pickled vegetables out of a vat. A cat hid crouching on the tattered asphalt felt roofing above their heads.

'Miss, are you getting off here?' asked the rickshaw puller.

Autumn Grace shook her head. 'No, just keep going.'

As the rickshaw passed her father, Autumn Grace pulled a square ring off her finger and dropped it into the bowl of beans. Her father didn't notice and continued to concentrate on stringing beans. Autumn Grace felt a gut-wrenching pain. She covered her face with her hands. 'Go. Keep going,' she said to the rickshaw puller.

'Where *do* you want to go, miss?' he asked.

'I told you to keep going,' Autumn Grace snapped. 'Are you worried I won't pay?'

Leaving the city behind them, golden yellow rapeseed

flowers appeared on both sides of the road. As Autumn Grace surveyed the pastoral scenes of spring, the black tiles and white walls of the Joyous Moon Priory became visible through the surrounding bamboo forest. She stood up in the rickshaw and pointed. 'What temple is that?' she asked the rickshaw puller.

'It's a Buddhist convent.'

Autumn Grace suddenly broke into a smile. 'Go there,' she said. 'I might as well shave my head and become a nun.'

Just as Autumn Grace approached the convent hauling her suitcase through the bamboo grove, two women, lay worshipers from the village, came out and eyed her suspiciously 'This is a rich pilgrim,' scoffed one.

Autumn Grace smiled at the women. She stood in front of Joyous Moon Priory's vermillion lacquered doors and turned her head to take in her shadow on the ground. In the twilight, her faint shadow appeared fragile. 'This is the place,' she said to herself, 'I'll shave my head and become a nun. And that will be that.'

A pine oil lamp on the altar table was the only source of light in the incense-filled priory hall. Autumn Grace saw two pale-faced nuns standing behind the statuary niche. One was still young but the other was very old. They coldly eyed Autumn Grace. 'The benefactor desires to make an offering of incense?'

Autumn Grace descended into the depths of infinite

darkness. Suffering from days of nervous exhaustion her body suddenly became limp when she arrived in the priory hall. She kneeled on a prayer mat and knocked her head on the ground in supplication to the two nuns.

'Please take me in. I have nowhere else to go.'

The nuns did not respond.

'Please let me stay here,' pleaded Autumn Grace. 'I have a lot of money. I can support all of you.'

The older nun rolled prayer beads between her fingers and rapidly recited some lines from a Buddhist sutra. The young nun, however, covered her mouth and furtively smiled.

Autumn Grace suddenly raised her head. Her eyes were filled with anxiety and despair. She pounded on the edge of the prayer mat with all her might and screamed: 'Are you both deaf? Can't you hear I am begging you? Let me become a nun. Let me stay here. If you don't answer me, I'll burn down this priory and none of us will get out alive.'

Autumn Grace would never forget her first night at Joyous Moon Priory. She slept alone in a small storeroom piled high with firewood and farm tools. A candle flickered on the windowsill. The night wind soughed through the bamboo grove outside, and later she heard the trickling of rain. She tossed and turned to the sound of the rain, thinking of how she slept beside Mr P'u just the previous evening. Overnight, the remnants of her old world filled with the scent of rouge powder lay out of reach, beyond the walls. Autumn Grace mused on her situation. *This world is truly treacherous and unpredictable. A person can live up to today and not know what will happen tomorrow. Who would have thought that Autumn Grace of Red Delight Pavilion would enter a convent?*

*

Much later, Petulia heard about Autumn Grace shaving her head to become a nun. That was when Mr P'u visited Petulia at the labour camp, and the first thing he told her was that Autumn Grace had entered a convent. Petulia was shocked and thought Mr P'u was joking. 'It's true,' said Mr P'u. 'I only recently found out myself. I went to visit her but she refused to see me.' Petulia fell silent and on the verge of tears, her eyes reddened.

'You must have mistreated her,' said Petulia. 'Otherwise, she would not have taken that path.'

Mr P'u looked thoroughly miserable. 'It's a long story,' he began. 'Things were difficult for me, too.'

'Autumn Grace was so good to you,' said Petulia.' 'That's rare for a girl from Emerald Cloud Lane. Do you understand, Mr P'u?'

'I know,' said Mr P'u. 'But now you are the only one who can persuade her to come back. She listens to you.'

A wry smile appeared on Petulia's face. 'Mr P'u,

you're talking nonsense again. How can I help? I won't get out of here for at least half a year, and that's only if I perform my tasks especially well, but I don't. I can only sew twenty sacks a day. I am sick of living, too.'

The two of them sat facing each other on two rocks below the guard tower, in silence. Visits were for only thirty minutes. Petulia looked up at the guard in the tower and said, 'Time is almost up. Mr P'u, please talk about something else.'

'What do you want me to talk about?' asked Mr P'u.

'Anything,' said Petulia, her head lowered to gaze at stones on the ground. 'Anything at all.'

Mr P'u vacantly stared at Petulia's pointy chin, then extended his hand to pet it. 'Petulia, poor girl, you're pitifully thin.'

Petulia's shoulders twitched and she turned away from him. 'I'm not to be pitied,' she said softly. 'I have reaped what I have sown. No one else is to blame.'

Mr P'u had more bad news for Petulia: The madam at Red Delight Pavilion had left the city and taken all of Petulia's possessions. Petulia looked at Mr P'u sadly. 'Left nothing at all?'

Mr P'u thought for a moment. 'I managed to scrounge a rouge tin in the doorway that looks like the one you used, and took it home.'

Petulia nodded. 'A rouge tin. Very well, you hold on to it for me.'

Despite her pitiful circumstances, Petulia quickly adjusted to life in the camp, as she was a resilient girl. Sewing hessian sacks helped restore her sleep and her chronic anxiety cured itself. At night, Lucky Phoenix's hands often crept under Petulia's blanket, caressing and kneading her breasts and thighs. Petulia was not bothered by it. She simply pushed Lucky Phoenix's hand away and went back to sleep.

But one night in a dream, Petulia saw a giant hand covered in black hair slowly caressing her body from head to toe. She woke up in a cold sweat, then realised it was Lucky Phoenix's hand touching her again. This time Petulia became annoyed. She pinched the back of Lucky Phoenix's hand hard.

'Don't touch me!' said Petulia. 'No one can touch me!'

The man's hand often emerged in front of Petulia's eyes when she was working in the warehouse. Sometimes the hand would float mid-air, sometimes it would emerge from nowhere and gently nibble like a fish at her private parts, leaving Petulia's face flushed while she was sewing sacks. She did not know whose hand it was, or what the hand represented, though she vaguely sensed the hand was a shadow of her past life.

In the spring of 1952, Petulia was notified that her reform through labour was complete, and she could leave the Women's Labour Training Institute and return to the city. Petulia was bewildered as soon as she heard the news and her skinny face became deathly pale again.

'Don't you want to get out of here?' asked a female cadre.

'It's not that. Just that I don't know what to do once I get out. I'm scared,' said Petulia.

'Now you can make an honourable living and be a new person,' said the cadre. 'We'll find you a job so you can also make contributions to the building of our motherland.'

The cadre then took out a stack of forms. 'Many factories are hiring female workers. Which one do you want to go to?' asked the cadre, pointing at the stack.

Petulia flipped through the forms. 'I don't know. I'll go to any place that doesn't require hard work.'

The female cadre sighed. 'I guess people like you can never be totally reformed. Go to the bottle-recycling factory, then. You really are a lazybones. Just go and sort glass bottles.'

*

In her early days in Joyous Moon Priory, Autumn Grace habitually sat in front of a mirror combing her hair. She noticed the face in the mirror was becoming paler by the day. A boil appeared on her lip. She ran her hand through her treasured hair, the hair that was soon to be shaven off. Realising her beauty as a woman would soon disappear together with her hair, Autumn Grace was overwhelmed by despair.

The prioress chose an auspicious day and time for Autumn Grace's ordination ceremony. Her hair would be shaved off and she would be given a Buddhist name. A pair of scissors, wrapped in red cloth, was placed on the altar. A young nun stood next to the altar holding a pan filled with clean water. Autumn Grace stared at the scissors while shielding her hair with her two hands. 'I don't want my hair shaved,' cried Autumn Grace suddenly. 'I treasure my hair.'

'Your affinity with *samsara*, the material world, is not over yet and you should not have come there. You must leave now,' said the prioress.

'I don't want to shave my hair. And I don't want to leave, either,' bleated Autumn Grace.

'That is not possible,' said the nun. 'Either you keep your hair and stay away from the Buddha, or you shave off your hair and take refuge in the Buddha. You must make a choice.'

Autumn Grace glared, stomped her feet and shouted: 'All right! You don't have to force me. I'll cut it myself!'

Then she grabbed the scissors from the altar with one hand, lifted her hair with the other, and cut. Tufts of black hair drifted down and landed on the floor of the priory. Autumn Grace cried and tried to catch strands of her hair mid-air.

Three days after Autumn Grace's ordination, Mr P'u's enquiries led him to Joyous Moon Priory. It was not a day of public worship and the priory gate was bolted shut. Mr P'u knocked on the gate for a long time, and the person who came to open it was none other than Autumn Grace. As soon as she saw it was Mr P'u, Autumn Grace quickly slammed the gate shut. 'Get lost!' she said.

At first, Mr P'u did not recognise Autumn Grace, and it was too late by the time he realised it was her.

'Don't open the gate, there's a thief outside,' Mr P'u heard Autumn Grace say to someone. He continued knocking on the gate but there was only silence on the other side.

Mr P'u did not want to give up. He walked to the back of the priory thinking he could climb over the wall. But the wall was too high for Mr P'u who had never in his life climbed over a wall, or even a through a window. All he could do was keep knocking and pushing on the gate. Eventually, he heard the bolt inside start to move, then the gate opened just slightly. Mr P'u poked his head through the gap and saw Autumn Grace standing behind the gate coldly glaring at him.

'Autumn Grace, finally I can see you again. Please, come home with me,' implored Mr P'u.

Autumn covered her head with her hands – it was almost an instinctive reaction. Mr P'u struggled to squeeze his shoulders through the gap of the gate.

'Autumn Grace, please! Open the gate,' pleaded Mr P'u. 'I have so much to tell you. And why did you shave off your hair? Things are alright now so you don't have to hide anymore. But why did you shave off your hair?'

Suddenly, Mr P'u's hand stretched out through the gap of the gate and grabbed Autumn Grace's black gown. Autumn Grace jumped as if she were burned.

'Don't touch me!' she screamed.

Mr P'u gazed in despair at Autumn Grace, who was still trying to cover her head with hands. 'Don't look at me!' she shrieked.

Mr P'u's hand waggled around trying to reach for Autumn Grace's hand. The gate was squeaking with Mr P'u's attempt to squeeze himself through. All of a sudden Autumn Grace picked up a wooden pole from behind the gate and lifted it up. 'Get out!' she bellowed. 'Go away, or I'll beat you to death!'

Mr P'u stood outside Joyous Moon Priory, disheartened. He could hear Autumn Grace crying behind the bolted gate. 'Autumn Grace, don't be so stubborn. Please come back with me,' he pleaded. 'If you want marriage, I'll give you marriage. Whatever you like.'

But Autumn Grace had already trudged away.

Mr P'u was surrounded by a deathly stillness, except for the sound of bamboo rustling in the wind and the intermittent barking of a dog in a village in the distance.

Joyous Moon Priory was only three miles away from the dazzling city, but it was not the same, after all.

That day, Mr P'u vowed to forget about Autumn Grace. He felt humiliated by the image of himself squeezing his head through the gate of Joyous Moon Priory and begging Autumn Grace. *There are plenty of full-figured women in this world, so what is the point of longing for Autumn Grace? After all, she's just another prostitute from Emerald Cloud Lane.*

In 1952, Mr P'u's extravagant lifestyle was decimated – the government confiscated all properties of the P'u family and the bank froze the enormous savings account inherited from Mr P'u's ancestors. Mr P'u was devastated. Every day he rested his head on his desk in the electric company, and snoozed. One day, he received a phone call from Petulia. She told Mr P'u that she had been released from the Training Institute and asked Mr P'u to accompany her to visit Autumn Grace.

'Why do you want to see her?' asked Mr P'u. 'She's half dead. You can come and see me, at least I'm still alive.'

Waiting at the entrance of the electricity company, Mr P'u saw Petulia leisurely walking towards him. She wore a fashionable double-breasted open collar blue Lenin suit fastened with a belt, and a pair of simple black cotton slip-ons. Apart from her flirtatious carriage and seductive glances, she looked just like any other woman on the street. Petulia stopped in front of

Mr P'u. Bathed in sunlight, she gave Mr P'u an alluring smile. Mr P'u suddenly was struck by the discovery that Petulia had become much prettier than the scrawny little waif he remembered.

It was lunchtime, so Mr P'u led Petulia towards the lively restaurant precinct.

'Petulia, what do you want to eat? Western food or Chinese food?'

'Western food. I crave pork and beef steaks, and stewed chicken. I haven't had a good meal in two years,' answered Petulia.

'All right, all right.' Mr P'u smiled while nervously rummaging his pockets. Times had changed – these days Mr P'u was often cash-strapped.

He estimated how much he had in his pocket and decided that he would have to skip lunch.

The two of them walked into the famous Penguin Bistro. Mr P'u ordered food only for Petulia and just a glass of 'Dutch water' – flavoured soda water – for himself.

Petulia put the napkin on her lap, elated. 'I'm already salivating.'

'Whatever makes you happy,' said Mr P'u. 'I ate lunch at the company. I will join you for a drink.'

Autumn Grace's name came up in conversation.

'I just can't believe it! How could a gregarious person like Autumn Grace become a nun?' said Petulia.

'Who knows. The world is a mess and everything's upside-down.'

Petulia pointed at Mr P'u's nose with her fork: 'It must've been you! You heartless bastard! Autumn Grace must hate you so much to have taken this path.'

Mr P'u gesticulated with open arms. 'She can hate me, but whom should I hate? I'm not doing so well either, and these days I can barely look after myself.' Petulia paused for a long moment then sighed. 'Poor Autumn Grace. But you're right – now we all have to look after ourselves.'

A waiter brought over the bill. Fortunately, Mr P'u had enough money to avoid making a spectacle of himself. He even tipped generously, like a real gentleman. Petulia hooked her arm in Mr P'u's when they left the restaurant. All sorts of feelings welled up in Mr P'u's mind when he thought about his own bleak situation – his dream life had come to an end. An impecunious man in front of a woman is a useless man.

They strolled together, each immersed in their own thoughts. Mr P'u accompanied Petulia all the way to her bottle-recycling factory. Petulia pointed at the bamboo-fenced factory compound. 'Look at this dreadful place,' Petulia lamented, 'It's mind-numbing!'

'Let's go to a dancehall next time,' said Mr P'u.

'Are there still dancehalls these days?' asked Petulia.

'Let's try to find one. Maybe some are still in business.'

Petulia tried a foxtrot dance step. 'Oh, no!' she cried. 'I can barely remember how to dance!' She raised her head to look at Mr P'u. Suddenly she thought about her friend. *What about Autumn Grace?* 'Forget about dancing for now. Take me to see Autumn Grace.'

Mr P'u shook his head in resentment. 'I'm not going,' he said. 'She left me stuck halfway through the gate and wouldn't let me in. If you want to go, you can go by yourself.'

'How can I go by myself?' said Petulia. 'I don't even know how to get there. And I don't have any money to buy her a gift. We don't have to go if you don't want to see her. Let's go dancing, then.'

Three days later Petulia and Mr P'u met up again. This time Mr P'u had money in his pocket, borrowed from his colleagues. They hired a rickshaw to pass through the business area of the city to seek out an entertainment establishment. The once lively dancehalls and bars had all disappeared like autumn leaves. By nightfall, the city looked deserted. Under dim neon lights, suspicious-looking vagrants lay curled up in blankets at street corners. Their rickshaw passed the archway of Emerald Cloud Lane, which now was covered in slogans and banners. The street hawkers were packing up their stalls and heading home.

'Quick! Go and buy some crystal buns! Or it'll be too late!' Petulia urged, pointing at the stalls.

Mr P'u jumped off the rickshaw and returned with some steamed buns wrapped in translucent dough. As he put his hand on the rickshaw, he gazed up at Red Delight Pavilion. The once brightly-lit establishment now was in darkness, like an abandoned movie set.

'Do you want to go back to take a look?' asked Mr P'u.

Petulia bit into a crystal bun, then mumbled, 'No, no, it'll only cause heartache.'

Mr P'u thought about it, then said, 'Yes, that's right. It'll only cause heartache.'

They continued to circle the city in search of a dancehall but eventually lost hope when the former owner of a dancehall, with whom Mr P'u had been acquainted, poked his head out of a window to impatiently wave them off as though they were birds. 'Go away! Go! Times have changed. Can't you see! All the eight famous dancehalls have been shut down! Dance? Go home and dance in bed!' the man yelled.

Mr P'u returned to the rickshaw, dejected.

'What should we do next?' he asked.

'I don't know. Up to you,' said Petulia.

Mr P'u thought about it for a moment then said, 'Let's go to my place. Where I live now is shabby and there is not much furniture, but I have managed to save a tin of German coffee and a gramophone. We can dance there, whatever style we like.'

'Alright, let's go,' said Petulia. 'Just don't bump into any other women,' she grinned coquettishly.

That year, Mr P'u had moved house several times, settling at last in the former garage of the electricity company. Petulia stood in the doorway and poked her head through the door to look inside. 'I never imagined that Mr P'u could have fallen on such hard times,' she sighed.

'Life is unpredictable,' Mr P'u replied. 'I consider myself lucky to still be alive.'

Petulia walked in, plopped down on the bed and kicked off her shoes. 'Mr P'u,' she asked, 'are you really living alone?'

Mr P'u closed the curtain, then turned towards Petulia. 'I've always lived alone. Mother has moved in with my sister, so now I'm even more alone.'

Petulia lounged in the bed flipping through a movie magazine. Suddenly, she looked up and saw Mr P'u staring at her.

'Why are you standing there like an idiot?' she sniggered. 'Put on some music so we can dance!'

'My gramophone is broken,' replied Mr P'u.

'Then make some coffee.'

'The stove fire has gone out.'

Petulia covered her face with the magazine and giggled. 'What's your problem, Mr P'u? Is this how you are going to entertain me?'

Mr P'u jumped into bed and grabbed Petulia's waist.

'I'll entertain you in bed!' said Mr P'u. He then turned off the bed lamp.

In the dark, Petulia hit Mr P'u with the magazine.

'Don't toy with me, Mr P'u,' she panted. 'I am indebted to Autumn Grace.'

'So what? Nowadays, we can only worry about ourselves,' said Mr P'u.

Slowly Petulia leaned backwards. Out of habit, her fingers pinched Mr P'u's back.

'Oh, Mr P'u! How will I ever be able to face Autumn Grace again?' she whimpered.

Mr P'u quickly sealed her lips with his dry and coarse tongue. They began to float in the darkness, in silence.

*

The glass bottle-recycling factory had about two dozen female workers, of whom at least half were former prostitutes from the brothels on Emerald Cloud Lane. They sat in a circle as far away as possible from workers who hailed from ordinary families. The work was simple: the women would pick out undamaged bottles from piles stacked up like little mountains and wash them. Then, the clean bottles were transported elsewhere to be reused. In those days many people were unfamiliar with such manual labour enterprises and called the glass bottle-recycling factory the prostitutes' workshop.

Petulia's job was to clean bottles. She would insert her brush, scrub around the inside once, pour out the water and scrub again until the green or brown bottles were sparkling clean.

Petulia listlessly performed her repetitive task. She found the work terribly boring but she knew full well that there was no other work anywhere that would be easier. Her monthly salary was only fourteen *yuan*, which was barely enough to get by on.

She was stunned the first time she received her pay packet. 'What can I do with this pittance?' she groused.

'Depends on what you want to use it for,' retorted the female factory manager. 'Of course, it can't compare with your previous income, but this money is clean, and it carries no shame.'

Petulia was a little embarrassed. 'What's this about clean and dirty?' she shot back. 'Money is money, people are people. Even the cleanest people need money, just like the dirtiest people. Who on earth doesn't like money?'

The factory manager eyed Petulia scornfully, then pointed to the other workers. 'They get the same pay, so how come they can make do?'

As soon as Petulia left the room she cursed the factory manager: 'Shining white, a pockmarked fright, what a disgusting face!'

The factory manager really did have a pockmarked

face, which Petulia had always considered the sign of a wily person, and she frequently mocked the factory manager. Somehow the factory manager, a sturdy woman from Shantung province, caught wind of it and was so furious she threw a glass bottle at Petulia. Then she rushed up to Petulia to drag her away from the other workers, grabbed Petulia's hair and smashed her head against a bamboo fence.

'I have a pockmarked face,' the factory manager raged, 'because I suffered in the Old Society. I had smallpox but couldn't afford to have it treated. You may have a pretty face but you are a whore, and down there you are so filthy that maggots grow, so who do you think you are to be bad-mouthing people!'

Petulia realised she had only herself to blame, so she did not resist, even though tears streamed down her face as the factory manager continued to smash her head against the bamboo fence.

The other women rushed over to break up the fight. 'Stay out of it,' cried Petulia. 'Let her kill me. I don't want to go on living.'

That evening Petulia visited Mr P'u in his garage again. As soon as she saw Mr P'u, she collapsed into his arms and began to sob.

'What's the matter, Petulia?'

'The woman with the pockmarked face hit me,' she whimpered.

'Why did she hit you?'

'I called her pock face behind her back.'

'Well why did you curse her behind her back?' asked Mr P'u, unable to suppress his laughter. 'You really are childish. You must understand you're not in Red Delight Pavilion anymore. Nowadays, you can't afford to be so reckless, because you'll only suffer in the end.'

Petulia continued to cry. 'The madam at the brothel never hit me. The customers never hit me. Even at the Training Institute, no one ever hit me. And now a pockmarked woman hits me. How can you expect me to let it go?'

'What do you have in mind?' asked Mr P'u.

Petulia grabbed Mr P'u's collar. 'Mr P'u, I am depending on you. I want you to thrash the pockmarked woman to teach her a lesson.'

Mr P'u grimaced. 'I've never hit anyone in my life, let alone a woman.'

Petulia's tone of voice changed as she frowned in anguish at Mr P'u. 'If you can stand idly by and watch me being bullied then you're not much of a man, are you, Mr P'u? Stop playing dumb! A real man would go and beat her up tomorrow.'

'Alright,' said Mr P'u, 'I'll find someone to give her a good thrashing.'

'No!' cried Petulia, 'I want *you* to do it. I'll only be satisfied if *you* beat her up.'

'Petulia, you really are a difficult one. I just can't win.'

Mr P'u thought Petulia's demand was ridiculous, but nonetheless, the next day he hid outside the glass bottle-recycling factory to ambush the pockmarked factory manager. Wearing a windbreaker and a surgical facemask, Mr P'u stood waiting for a long time. Finally, he saw a woman with pockmarks all over her face come out, and when she turned to lock the gate Mr P'u stepped forward. 'Excuse me,' he said.

When the woman turned, Mr P'u punched her in the face.

'What are you doing?' she shrieked.

'Shut up!' barked Mr P'u. 'I'm almost done.'

Mr P'u then pinched her buttocks and ran off.

'Hooligan!' she suddenly screamed from behind him. 'Arrest the hooligan!'

Mr P'u was scared out of his wits, and bolted up a lane for all he was worth. Luckily, there was no one about. It would have been very embarrassing if someone had caught up with him.

Mr P'u eventually stopped to catch his breath. He thought about how absurd it must have looked, and that perhaps he should not have pinched the woman's buttocks, because that could give the mistaken impression he had waited at the gate to grope the pockmarked woman. Mr P'u began to pity himself: *I have really suffered a lot because of women.*

Mr P'u returned to the garage. The door was ajar. Petulia was cutting her toenails in bed. She quickly slid back under the blanket as soon as she saw Mr P'u.

'Where did you stray off to?' she demanded.

'Didn't you tell me to teach pock face a lesson?' said Mr P'u. 'I went and punched her so hard her face was black and blue and she fell to the ground.'

Petulia chuckled. 'Mr P'u, you really are gullible. I just wanted to find out if you really cared about me. Who would have expected you to actually go and punch her!'

Mr P'u stood frozen watching Petulia choke in hilarity. *How did I let her make a fool of me! I let her play me like an idiot! Almost made a spectacle of myself!*

'You mad bitch!' he cursed.

Finally, Petulia had enough of laughter. She patted the blanket and summoned Mr P'u. 'Come here. It's my turn to let you have your payback!'

Mr P'u, still fuming, walked over and pulled off Petulia's blanket to discover she had been stark naked all along. He pinched her hard. 'I'll fix you,' said Mr P'u, gnashing his teeth. 'I won't stop today until you beg for mercy!'

Petulia playfully scraped Mr P'u's nose with her finger. 'Well, let's see if you can,' she teased.

The faint yellow light slowly faded and the room eventually sank into darkness. A sweet-fishy odour lingered in the air. Neither of them wanted to get out of bed.

Suddenly, *bang!* Something hit the window. Mr P'u jumped out of bed and opened the curtain to check. Two little boys outside were throwing stones for fun. Mr P'u stroked himself on his chest. 'Phew! Scared me out of my wits! I thought someone was here to catch us in the act.'

'Who was that?' asked Petulia, still in bed. 'Surely, it couldn't be Autumn Grace?'

'No, just two boys.'

Petulia hopped out of bed and urinated into an enamel basin that was on the floor.

'That's my wash basin!' Mr P'u yelped.

'So what?' said Petulia still squatting. 'I'll pour it out in a moment.'

Then she stood up and quickly poured her urine into the garage's drainage ditch.

'Oh no!' Mr P'u yelped again. 'You just poured it onto my leather shoes!'

He ran over to rescue his shoes that he usually tossed into the ditch. But it was too late – they were already soaked. He hurled the shoes into a corner of the garage.

'What do you think were you doing? What will I wear tomorrow?'

'Buy a pair of new shoes, then,' said Petulia nonchalantly.

Mr P'u smiled wryly at her. 'Easy for you to say. These

days I don't even know where my next meal is coming from. Where will I get the money to buy leather shoes?' said Mr P'u.

Sensing Mr P'u was genuinely cross, Petulia became annoyed too. She pouted her lips and countered, 'Mr P'u, are you a real man? How could you blow up at me like that over a pair of silly old shoes!'

Then she sat in silence.

Mr P'u morosely turned on the light and dressed himself. Looking at Petulia covered with a pillowslip facing away from him as though she were about to cry, Mr P'u realised he could never win. He walked over to Petulia and helped her get dressed, and her tears instantly transformed into laughter. 'I'm hungry,' she declared.

'Well if you're hungry, let's go out to eat,' said Mr P'u.

'Where to? How about the Szechuan place?'

'Let's go out first, then we'll see.'

Mr P'u fished his gold watch out from under a pillow. He sighed. 'I wonder how much I can get for this?'

'You want to pawn your gold watch?'

'I have to. I don't have a penny to my name,' he said. 'Don't you dare tell anyone. If it gets out, I'll lose face.'

'That would be terrible.' Petulia frowned. 'We can skip one meal.'

Mr P'u grabbed Petulia's hand. 'Let's go!' he insisted. 'Don't worry so much. I've always said, "Today we have wine, so today we'll get drunk. Who cares if tomorrow we live or die".'

The two of them left the garage arm in arm. Outside, puddles had formed on the ground because it had just rained, though inside the garage they had been completely oblivious to everything around them. The wind added to the autumnal atmosphere. Petulia hugged herself and walked a few steps, then suddenly stopped.

'Now what?' queried Mr P'u.

Petulia raised her head to look at the trees lining the road and the deep blue night sky above the branches. 'It's getting cold,' she said. 'It will soon be winter.'

'Nothing we can do about that,' said Mr P'u. 'Winter always follows autumn.'

'I'm scared,' said Petulia. 'How will I ever survive a winter alone in the factory dormitory? There's no heater and I don't have padded silk robes anymore. How will I get through the winter?'

'Don't worry about the cold,' said Mr P'u. 'I'll warm you in my arms.'

Petulia looked at Mr P'u then lowered her eyes. 'This is the New Society, we can't be together like this without proper status,' she said. 'Mr P'u, why don't you marry me?'

Mr P'u stopped dead in his tracks. 'Marriage is a good thing, but I'm afraid I can't support you now. When I should have married I didn't want to, and now that

I want to get married, I can't. Surely, you know I'm a penniless pauper now.'

Petulia broke into a charming smile and hooked her arm into Mr P'u's. 'Someone like me only deserves a penniless pauper, wouldn't you say?'

*

Mr P'u spent the rest of the autumn running from friend to friend and relative to relative to borrow money for his wedding to Petulia. He promised Petulia they would have a proper wedding, rent a place of their own, and that Petulia would no longer have to work at the glass bottle-recycling factory. It would all take money. But most important of all: Petulia was already pregnant. Only the strongest and most virile men can make a girl from Emerald Cloud Lane pregnant, he vaguely recalled someone as saying, and he felt an overwhelming tinge of pride.

Very few people were willing to lend Mr P'u any money. Relatives would either cold shoulder him or put on a sorry face. Mr P'u knew their unspoken message was: *You are a notorious wastrel. Lending money to you is like using silver ingots as skipping stones on water. We can't afford that.*

He would politely depart, somewhat embarrassed, leaving behind the pastries he had brought with him as gifts. Mr P'u would never pester or beg. He always maintained his usual courteous manner of the privileged, even when he was in dire straits. But privately, he bemoaned the fickleness of human nature – in the old days, when the P'u family was still rolling in money, these people fell over themselves in sycophantic flattery. Now they just wanted to run away from him as if he were infected with the plague.

Mr P'u was down to his last resort – to ask for help from his mother. He had wanted to hide his relationship with Petulia from Mrs P'u because he knew she definitely would not sanction their marriage. But under the circumstances, he had no choice but to confess to his mother.

Bearing yet another box of pastries, Mr P'u set off to his older sister's home.

As expected, Mrs P'u was so enraged she threatened to kill herself as soon as she learned about Mr P'u's relationship with Petulia.

'You just want to see me die!' she wailed, pointing her finger at Mr P'u's nose. 'You are the scion of a good family. Why are you consorting with whores? I'm not giving you a penny. You might as well just kill me!'

'Petulia is a good girl. We'll be a good couple once we're married,' said Mr P'u, patiently defending his decision.

'A whore is always a whore, no matter how good she

is! Do you really think a woman like that would be a good wife?' sneered Mrs P'u.

'Mother, I'm begging you. Petulia is already pregnant.'

'Pregnant?' Mrs P'u snorted. 'She certainly is a crafty one. Why must the continuation of the P'u family line depend on a whore?'

Mr P'u was so desperate that his face turned flaming red and his voice became hoarse. 'I have nowhere else to go. Do you want me to kneel down in front of you and beg?'

In the end, Mrs P'u collapsed into a rattan armchair and wailed. Mr P'u found his mother's harrowing reaction a little revolting.

Why all this drama? It's not like I'm a murderer or an arsonist. All I want is to marry Petulia from Emerald Cloud Lane. Why can't I marry a prostitute? My heart is set on Petulia, and no one can do anything about it.

In the end, Mrs P'u handed her son a metallic cigarette case, inside which was five gold ingots. She coldly glared at him. 'This is everything the P'u family has. Take it and do whatever you like. If you squander it all, don't come back to me – you are no longer my son.'

Mr P'u slipped the cigarette case into his pocket and smiled at his mother. 'If you don't want me to come here again, then I won't. I don't need to suckle your milk anymore.'

In the winter of 1953, Mr P'u and Petulia held their

wedding banquet in a hotel famous throughout southern China. Although the families from both sides were not in attendance, the guests who came nonetheless filled the banquet hall. Mr P'u invited all the employees of the electric company, and for her part, Petulia invited all the girls from her former days at Emerald Cloud Lane.

The wedding was a truly extravagant event, though rather than being an exhibition of habitual self-indulgence, it was more of a meticulously staged enjoyment. Mr P'u knew full well that this would be his last hurrah. His colleagues from the electricity company noticed that despite his exuberant demeanour, Mr P'u appeared to be burdened with grief. Petulia, on the other hand, enrobed in a white wedding dress, radiantly glided amongst the guests, charming all with her seductive glamour. Petulia's background was no secret to the guests. But after objective conjecture, they concluded that the marriage was a matter of course.

Weddings are always joyful occasions that eclipse the vulgar talk of men and the secret suspicions of women. The former prostitutes of Emerald Cloud Lane saw the changes in Petulia's physique and knowingly congratulated her with doubled-edged compliments: 'Petulia, what a happy event! You're so lucky!'

While Petulia was graciously entertaining the wedding guests, a waiter came forward with a red fabric bundle. 'A nun has brought you this. She says it is your dowry.'

Petulia unwrapped the bundle. Inside was a purple, satin-covered jewellery box, which contained a dragon-phoenix bracelet. Autumn Grace's name stood out as plain as day. Petulia's face blanched a deathly pale. 'Where is she?' she asked the waiter in a timorous voice.

'She's gone,' he replied. 'She said she hadn't been invited.'

Petulia bunched up her wedding dress and ran outside, repeatedly calling, 'Autumn Grace, my beloved sister.'

Wedding guests who did not know what had happened, stood up to watch.

Mr P'u dismissively waved his hand. 'It's nothing. Her sister has come from the countryside, that's all.'

The more knowledgeable female guests nearby covered their mirth with their hands and loudly asked, 'That was Autumn Grace, wasn't it?'

Mr P'u blushed. 'Yes, it was. As you know, she entered a priory.'

Petulia ran out of the hotel. She saw Autumn Grace in a black gown standing under a street light on the other side of the road. Petulia raced across the road but Autumn Grace began to run too, her black robe rustling in the wind.

Petulia stood in the middle of the road. 'Autumn Grace,' she called out, 'Please don't run. Listen to me.'

Autumn Grace did not look back.

'Go back to your wedding,' Autumn Grace called out. 'And don't say anything.'

Petulia ran a few steps, then squatted down, covered her face with her hands and began to cry. 'Autumn Grace, why aren't you cursing me? You should have been the one who married Mr P'u, so why don't you curse me?'

Autumn Grace stopped in front of an umbrella store. She watched Petulia crying in the distance with total indifference. When Petulia stopped crying and raised her head, Autumn Grace spoke. 'What's there to curse? No shortage of men in this world and Mr P'u is not the only man. I can't really get married until my hair grows back. I just want you to promise that you will be good to Mr P'u. He has been kind to you, so you must be kind to him, too.'

Petulia tearfully nodded her assent. She then watched Autumn Grace buy an umbrella in the shop and stand there opening and closing the umbrella. 'Why did I buy an umbrella? It's not raining. What will I use it for?' said Autumn Grace to herself. Suddenly, she threw the umbrella towards Petulia. 'Take it. I'm giving the two of you this umbrella. If it rains, you may use it.'

Petulia caught the umbrella. 'Autumn Grace, my dear sister, come back with me, I have so much to tell you.'

Autumn Grace regarded Petulia with a calm glint in her eyes. But that glint quickly turned piercingly cold. She stared at Petulia's belly and snorted sardonically:

'Conceived for Mr P'u have you? You *are* a fast worker.'

Petulia began to sob again. 'I had no choice, Mr P'u hounded me and I became entangled.'

Autumn Grace spat contemptuously. 'He entangled you, or you entangled him? Don't take me for a fool. Do you think I don't know what you are? You were born a slut, and will always be a slut.'

Autumn Grace's black robe soon melted into the darkness. Petulia felt it was all so surreal. She and Mr P'u had almost forgotten about Autumn Grace. Maybe it was their intention, or maybe it was meant to be that way. Sometimes, men are like buses that women have to hitch a ride on. Whoever gets on the bus will move on with life. Petulia thought Autumn Grace should not be angry at her, and there was no use of being angry at her anyway – now she and Mr P'u were already married.

Petulia walked back to the hotel, umbrella in hand. Mr P'u and a few guests were waiting at the entrance. Petulia adjusted her hairpin and wedding dress, then put on a smile. 'Let's go back in. I was just seeing her off,' said Petulia calmly.

Just as Petulia arrived the hotel entrance, she suddenly sensed there was something ominous about the umbrella in her hand. *The word* san, *umbrella, sounds the same as the word for separation. What does it mean to give me an umbrella on my wedding day? Is it a curse on my marriage?*

Petulia immediately hurled the umbrella onto the street. A passing truck crushed the umbrella, emitting brittle sounds: *Crack! Crack!*

*

Mr P'u and Petulia's marital home was two rented rooms on the ground floor of a two-story house. The landlords were a couple who lived upstairs. They were *p'ing-t'an* musical performers. Every morning they practised singing, with the husband playing the moon-shaped *yüeh-ch'in* lute and his wife playing the pear-shaped pipa lute. Their usual storytelling ballad was the opening of *Lin Ch'ung Flees by Night,* about a legendary figure adapted from the novel the *Water Margin.*

Both Mr P'u and Petulia liked to sleep in. They were annoyed at being woken up every morning by the singing but found it hard to make a fuss. They just listened, and could not refrain from exchanging commentaries.

'Mr Chang is not bad. Listen! His voice is so resonant,' said Petulia.

'Mrs Chang is good. Her singing is so expressive,' said Mr P'u.

Petulia nudged Mr P'u with her elbow. 'You can just listen to her if she's that good!'

'You can just listen to him if *he* is that good!' Mr P'u countered.

They burst into laughter at the same time, realising both of them were harbouring suspicious thoughts.

As time went by, Mr P'u noticed Mr Chang's furtive glances always lingered inappropriately on Petulia's body. When Petulia went out in the morning to empty the chamber pot, he always followed her, pretending to pick up the daily paper. Once, Mr P'u spotted Mr Chang resting his hand on Petulia's buttocks for at least five seconds while saying something to her. Then he saw Petulia giggle.

Mr P'u felt like he had just swallowed a swarm of flies. As soon as Petulia returned, a livid Mr P'u demanded, 'What's going on between you and Mr Chang? You think I can't see, do you?'

'Come on, don't be jealous for no good reason. He was just telling me a joke. Mr Chang likes to tell jokes.'

'A joke?' Mr P'u sneered. 'What sort of joke can he tell?'

'A dirty joke,' Petulia tittered. 'It was hilarious and I almost died laughing. Want to hear it?'

'No! I'm not interested in his jokes. But I'm telling you, don't get too close to him. Or else!' Mr P'u bellowed.

'What are you talking about?' said Petulia, pouting her lips. 'I'm already yours! Besides, with my bulging belly, how could I sleep with him even if I wanted to?'

'Luckily you have a bulging belly. Otherwise, you would have slept with him ages ago,' snapped Mr P'u.

'Since I am at the office all day, you two can get up to whatever mischief you like.'

Petulia stood in a trance for a long moment. Suddenly, she burst into tears and dashed to grab a rope from behind the bed head. 'You wrong me! Now I will die before your eyes!' she wailed.

Mr P'u was horrified. He jumped over to seize the rope and threw it out the window.

The melodrama endured for the entire day. Mr P'u had to take the day off work to comfort Petulia. Tears streaming down Petulia's pretty face melted away his anger. He carried her to bed and held her in his arms. Sweet words gushed out. He was so moved by his own soliloquies that he himself was on the verge of tears. Gently, melancholically, Mr P'u's hand stroked her face, her neck, her breasts and eventually arrived at her bulging belly.

'Please don't cry,' pleaded Mr P'u. 'How will I live if something happens to you?'

Petulia finally stopped sobbing. She placed Mr P'u's hand on her face to caress herself and said, 'You are all I have. No one, not even my father or my mother, ever loved me. All I have is my man. If you don't care about me, all I can do is to die in front of you.'

That winter was bleak and endlessly long. Petulia often sat next the stove dozing. Random thoughts flashed across her mind. Outside the window, she could see the solitary French plane tree in the yard. The leaves had fallen long ago and all that remained were entangled branches quivering in the wind.

There was not much to see outside the window so Petulia spent long hours staring into the mirror. Having given up work at the bottle-recycling factory, she languished at home with nothing to do. She soon became visibly plump, and pregnancy caused her waist to spread. Disappointed with her appearance, Petulia seldom went out. The Chang household upstairs, however, seemed to be a constant hive of activity. Guests arrived every few days, bringing the sounds of laughter and conversation, and the clatter of footsteps. Petulia became inexplicably jealous and resentful. She did not like her lonely life, she hoped that she too could have visitors.

One day, Mr Chang called down to Petulia to come upstairs to play mahjong. Petulia cheerfully ascended the stairs and was confronted with a crowd of men and women surreptitiously sizing her up. She walked over to the mahjong table with unruffled grace.

Whenever Mr Chang mischievously called out 'brassiere' to refer to twin circle mahjong tiles, Petulia covered her mouth with her hand to hide her amusement. Whenever someone offered her a cigarette, she gladly accepted and blew almost perfect smoke rings.

Petulia was elated to be playing that day and did not return to her room downstairs until the early hours of the morning. She made her way in darkness towards the bed but Mr P'u tightly wrapped himself in the comforter and would not let her in. 'It's not yet light,' said Mr P'u in the darkness, 'go back and play some more.'

'What's wrong with playing a bit of mahjong? I'm stuck at home all day and hardly ever get a chance to play. What are you so angry about?'

'I slave away at the office to make money to feed my family and am not even greeted with a cup of hot tea. You've got it good, fondling mahjong tiles till the wee hours.'

Petulia lifted up the covers and caressed Mr P'u's manhood. 'Oh come on, my dear, don't be angry. I won't play mahjong anymore. I depend on you. I can't afford to make you angry.'

Mr P'u rolled over and sighed.

'Why are you sighing? You're my man so of course, you have to make money to look after me. There are no more brothels, otherwise, I'd be able to make some money to look after you, and wouldn't have to put up with your dirty looks.'

Mr P'u extended his arm to bang on the bed board. 'Enough!' he shouted. 'The more you say the worse it sounds. And it sounds to me like you can't let go of your old profession.'

Mr P'u's temper deteriorated greatly after the wedding. Petulia considered the reasons one by one, and discounted them all. Then she thought it might be because she was pregnant and was unable to fulfil her marital duties. Petulia concluded it was all the fault of the child in her belly. When she thought about the numerous little pleasures pregnancy had curtailed, she vented her anger on the unborn child. There are good and bad aspects to everything, but this point thoroughly deviated from the fantasy of marriage Petulia had cherished.

*

In the two years of her monastic life in Joyous Moon Priory, Autumn Grace had only returned to the city twice. Once was when she heard that Petulia and Mr P'u were to marry; the second time was when she received a letter from her aunt notifying her of the death of her father. The letter recounted how her father had been sitting just outside the house enjoying the sun when a car hit him, and he went flying through the air, never to wake up again.

Autumn Grace rushed home for her father's funeral. She cried the whole time she dutifully kept watch at his deathbed as befitted a filial daughter. She cried herself hoarse and was unable to speak for days. She knew half of her tears were for the departing spirit and the other half were for herself. She slept for two full days and nights after completing the funeral arrangements. She dreamt Petulia and Mr P'u were dancing on a vast roof of a house while she sobbed piteously in a dark corner, and then her dead father sat up in his coffin to cry with her. Autumn Grace cried herself awake. She thought about the dream for a long time, and concluded it represented nothing but weakness and unburdening, and that it was of little significance.

Autumn Grace's aunt held out a ring. 'I take it this is yours. I found it while stir-frying broad beans.' Autumn Grace nodded, recalling the occasion she passed by the family home but did not enter. Her eyes teared up. 'When are you returning to the priory?' asked her aunt. 'I made you a jar of pickled vegetables, the kind you like.'

Autumn Grace glanced at her aunt. 'You mean I *must* return to the priory? What if I don't want to be a nun anymore?'

'I'm not banishing you to the priory,' said her aunt a little embarrassed. 'This is your home, after all, and whether or not you return is entirely up to you.'

'I want you to tell me the truth,' said Autumn Grace, turning to face her aunt. 'Do you want me to stay?'

Her aunt hesitated for a moment. 'Better go back,' she said softly. 'Since you became a nun, the neighbours have had no excuse to bad-mouth our family.'

Autumn Grace blankly stared out the window at the run-down neighbourhood. She did not move as tears silently streamed down her cheeks. After a while, she bit her lip and spoke. 'You're right,' she said, 'it's better for me to go back. People outside the priory have had their hearts eaten by dogs.'

Autumn Grace returned to the priory the next day in mourning sackcloth. The young nun opened the gate but immediately shut it again as soon as she saw Autumn Grace.

'Open the gate!' Autumn Grace shouted. 'It's me! I'm back!'

She heard the young nun calling the prioress. 'Autumn Grace is back. You tell her.'

Perplexed by the young nun's reaction, Autumn Grace pounded on the gate as hard as she could. After a while, the prioress came.

'What have you come back for?' said the prioress scornfully from behind the closed gate. 'You lied to us. How dare a filthy woman like you enter the gate of this priory! Shameless! You've blemished Buddhism! Go! Go back to wherever you came from.' Autumn Grace screamed and pounded the gate with her fists. 'I don't understand this nonsense! Let me in! Open the gate!'

Clunk! The prioress bolted the gate from the inside. 'We have already lustrated the priory with clean water. You may not re-enter. You've done enough to besmirch the Joyous Moon Priory.'

Autumn Grace suddenly realised that she was destined by fate to fall into an abyss of despair. A wave of hopelessness engulfed her. Her body sagged lower and lower. Again and again, she hit the gate with her forehead, as she choked on her own tears.

'Please! Let me in!' she pleaded, sobbing convulsively. 'Please! I don't want to go back. People outside the priory have had their hearts eaten by dogs and I have nowhere else to go. Please! Take me in one more time.'

Autumn Grace pushed the front gate of Joyous Moon Priory so hard that it was about to give way. A dog inside barked hysterically.

'Go!' said the prioress. 'We wouldn't be able to feed you anyway. Now there are fewer donors and we have less food. An extra mouth means less food for us.'

'I have money! I can support you all!' Autumn Grace cried out. 'Don't worry about having less food to eat because of me. The food my money can buy will last longer than all of us!'

'You can just keep your filthy money to yourself,' Then the sound of footsteps gradually faded as the prioress trudged away. The dog stopped barking.

Eventually, Autumn Grace was once again surrounded by a silent void that was too deep for her tears.

In nearby bamboo groves, some peasants who were harvesting winter bamboo shoots witnessed this scene in front of the priory gate. They saw Autumn Grace's ashen face and her black-and-white robes of mourning fluttering in the wind as though broken-hearted. Then they saw Autumn Grace frantically collecting twigs and branches and piling them in front of the gate of Joyous Moon Priory. The peasants guessed she was about to light a fire. They watched anxiously, exchanging views about whether Autumn Grace could start a fire.

But Autumn Grace did not start a fire, or perhaps she lacked the courage to actually set the priory alight. Autumn Grace sat on the pile of firewood for a long time, her hands on her cheeks, deep in thought. She looked haggard but still was beautiful.

The peasants in the bamboo grove continued to watch Autumn Grace. 'I heard she was once a prostitute,' said one. Then the peasants saw Autumn Grace stand up, remove her black mourning robe, tear it into strips and tie it to the doorknocker. Beneath the robe, Autumn Grace wore a close-fitting blue brocade tunic with red flowers. The colours were brilliant. She stood in front of Joyous Moon Priory, looked around and quickly composed herself. The peasants later saw Autumn Grace carrying a small bundle, swinging her waist as she walked quietly past the bamboo grove. They could no longer see any trace of despair on her face.

*

By 1954, the government no longer pursued the former prostitutes inherited from the Old Society with much vigour. The Women's Labour Training Institutes set up specially to hold prostitutes were mostly closed. Autumn Grace, however, was disappointed to hear the news. *Why did I bother to go to such trouble to hide? Life is unpredictable. If I had not jumped off the army truck I would have gone together with Petulia to the labour camp. Perhaps I would not have found myself in this dead end.*

When Autumn Grace arrived home, her aunt was shocked. 'You really are back here for good, and won't return to the priory?'

Autumn Grace tossed her small bundle of possessions onto the bed. 'I'm not going back,' she said. 'I'm sick of being a nun. I thought I might as well come home to live a normal life.'

Her aunt's face darkened. 'How can there be a normal life for you here? You are accustomed to the dissolute life. What will the future hold for you?'

'Don't worry,' replied Autumn Grace. 'I'll get married soon enough. I just need a man who is willing to marry me, and I don't care who he is.'

'And after you're married?' said her aunt. 'Are you capable of being a good wife?'

'Of course, I am,' Autumn Grace grinned. 'As the saying goes, "If you marry a chicken follow the chicken, if you marry a dog follow the dog." If others can be content with the people they marry, then why can't I?'

Her aunt's family was visibly cold towards Autumn Grace, and Autumn Grace in return did not hide her hostility. No matter what she was doing, she did it grumpily. She did not care, so she had nothing to fear. Except once, while sweeping the floor she noticed part of a photograph buried in a pile of rubbish. She bent down to pick up the photo and cried. It was a picture of herself. It had been torn off a family group photo. The Autumn Grace in the photo, only eight or nine years old, was wearing her hair in two thin braids, her eyes wide open with fear, staring at the camera.

With the torn photo in hand, her whole body shook uncontrollably as she kicked open the door of her aunt's room. 'Who did this?' she screeched, brandishing the photo. 'Who hates me that much?'

Her aunt was not in. Only a younger cousin was there doing some woodwork with a carpenters plane.

'I did,' he replied, casting a disdainful glance at Autumn Grace. 'I hate you.'

'Why do you hate me?' asked Autumn Grace. 'I've never hurt you.'

'Why did you bother to come back? I can't get married because you now occupy the room!' her cousin replied. 'You were perfectly fine with whoring around all those years, so why come back and pretend to be respectable. You've only brought chaos to this household.'

Autumn Grace stood momentarily silent. Suddenly

she feigned a smile. 'Well, at least you are honest. But you don't know me. If you've got something to say, say it nicely. If one of you riles me, I will bury a clean blade in that someone, and pull out a red one.'

The expression on her cousin's face changed quickly – he immediately grinned from ear to ear. 'In that case, dear cousin, let's talk. Please hurry up and marry. If you don't have any candidates in mind, allow me to be your matchmaker. There's Feng the Fifth on East Street who has expressed an interest in you.'

'Shut your stinking mouth,' Autumn Grace squawked. 'I have plenty of experience whoring myself, so I certainly don't need you to teach me.' She violently shoved open the front door and stormed out of the house.

The wintry streets were deserted. Autumn Grace trudged beside the walls backing the street. She restlessly tapped her fingers on the walls and shutters of closed shops. Not only were the streets empty, she felt the entire world was empty. She plodded down Emerald Cloud Lane. Autumn Grace could never forget this narrow lane. She used to walk up and down, and back and forth along the laneway before finally entering Red Delight Pavilion, hoping a rich and handsome man would buy her virginity. She had turned down many men before Mr P'u arrived on the scene.

If at the age of sixteen Autumn Grace crossed a river, then Mr P'u was that solitary bridge. Autumn Grace could never forget the lasting impression he had made upon her.

In those days, everyone in Emerald Cloud Lane knew Autumn Grace. A few years had passed and society had undergone profound changes. Now, no one even made a passing glance at her, nor recognised that she was Autumn Grace of Red Delight Pavilion.

Autumn Grace wandered past a mutton shop and heard someone inside call out her name. It was Lucky Phoenix, Autumn Grace recognised her instantly. Lucky Phoenix ran out of the shop. 'Is it really you?' she said as she grabbed Autumn Grace's hand. 'Didn't you enter a priory?'

'I didn't feel like staying there, so I left,' said Autumn Grace.

'I always said you would come back sooner or later,' chirped Lucky Phoenix, clapping her hands. 'How could a girl from Red Delight Pavilion ever survive in a priory?' Lucky Phoenix laughed gaily. 'Where were you going?' she then asked.

'Nowhere really,' replied Autumn Grace. 'Just on the prowl for a husband.'

Lucky Phoenix laughed knowingly and dragged Autumn Grace into the mutton shop to have a bowl of soup.

Lucky Phoenix was married to the owner of the mutton shop. Autumn grace cast a quick glance at the man slicing chilled mutton cakes. He was a little plump but appeared to be a decent man. 'All right, then,' said Autumn Grace. 'You've all found your way into respectable households, and now I'm the only one left, an inferior cut, destined for a chopping board who knows where.'

'You sound so miserable,' said Lucky Phoenix. 'You were very popular once. So many men chased you and you could take your pick.'

'The past is past,' said Autumn Grace. She lowered her head and drank her mutton soup in silence.

Suddenly, Lucky Phoenix remembered something. 'That's right, I forgot to tell you, Petulia has had a son. Nine pounds. Did you receive red eggs from the family celebrating the birth?'

Autumn Grace faintly smiled and shook her head in silence. After a while she asked, 'Are they getting on well?'

'Not at all,' said Lucky Phoenix. 'I've heard they're always fighting. You know Petulia has a short fuse, always threatening to do herself in. I don't think she'll die, but I fear she will be the death of Mr P'u.'

'Nothing can be done about that,' said Autumn Grace, lowering her head. 'Everything is preordained.'

'Do you want to see them?' asked Lucky Phoenix.

Autumn Grace shook her head again. 'I saw them once at the wedding,' she replied. 'That was enough.'

When Autumn Grace was saying her goodbyes, Lucky Phoenix enquired about the wedding date. Autumn Grace thought for a moment. 'Soon,' she said.

'If I just make do, it will be very soon.'

'Don't forget to let us know,' said Lucky Phoenix. 'We're all sisters. We must go to your wedding.'

'We'll see,' said Autumn Grace. 'Depends on who I marry.'

In half a month Autumn Grace married Feng the Fifth from East Street, but she did not invite anyone. Many months later, someone spotted Autumn Grace cleaning a chamber pot in the public toilet on East Street. A little pigeon-chested man with a hunchback was standing behind her. Her former colleagues from Emerald Cloud Lane were astonished when they learned the news of her marriage to a hunchback. They could not believe Autumn Grace would entrust the rest of her life to a man like that. Eventually, they concluded that Autumn Grace must be so heartbroken that she had simply written herself off by marrying whoever was available. They were all convinced that Autumn Grace's true love was Mr P'u, but Petulia had snatched him away.

*

Mr P'u named his son Griever.

'This name is no good,' said Petulia. 'It sounds dreadful. Why not 'Sunny' or something else?'

Mr P'u waved his hand dismissively. 'I want to call him Griever. It's meaningful.'

Petulia frowned. 'What do you mean by that?' she asked.

Mr P'u picked up his son and gazed at the baby's face. 'It means what it means. Griever – growing up with nothing but grief, so much grief there can be no tears.'

Following tradition, Petulia was confined at home for a month after giving birth. Mr P'u hired a nursemaid from the countryside to look after the new mother and to wash diapers. Mr P'u could not handle these chores, and he did not want to, either. He had to grit his teeth to hire the maid and borrow money to pay her.

A month passed. Knowing the money he had would not be enough to feed a household of four, Mr P'u steeled himself to fire the maid.

Petulia had not known about Mr P'u's decision. She waited in bed for the maid to serve her poached eggs, but the maid did not come. Petulia pounded the bed and yelled, 'Why aren't you bringing me my food? Do you want to starve me to death?'

Mr P'u entered the room holding two eggs. 'Get up and cook them yourself. I've fired the maid.'

'What's wrong with you?' Petulia demanded. 'Why didn't you talk to me about firing the maid? I just gave birth and you're asking me to cook for myself?'

'We all would starve if I hadn't fired her. You know we were running out of money.'

Petulia darted a suspicious glance at Mr P'u. 'There

were five gold ingots! Who knows what you squandered them on.'

Mr P'u's eyes opened wide and filled with rage as he craned his neck forward. 'Nowadays, I don't gamble, I don't whore and I don't spend a penny on myself!' he shouted. 'It's all because of you! You wanted good food, you wanted good clothes, and now you're blaming me!'

Petulia knew she was in the wrong but did not want to admit it. She slid back under the blanket and countered, 'Who else is to be blamed? You're the one who is useless and can't make big money.'

'You think we still live in the Old Society? These days everyone has to live on their salaries. Where is the big money to be made? Unless I rob the bank or embezzle company funds, you'd better stop even dreaming about living like a wife of someone who has money to throw around!'

Petulia was still unwilling to get up and do any housework, so Mr P'u had to throw together some things to eat and delivered them to her bedside. They were always either too salty or too bland. Petulia frowned as she ate his offerings. Sometimes she simply pushed the food aside and ate nothing.

In the end, Mr P'u could take no more. He smashed the bowl to the ground. 'Don't want to eat? Fine!' Mr P'u barked. 'I don't have anyone to serve me! Will your post-confinement rest ever end?'

Petulia and the infant in her arms burst into tears in

unison. Whenever Petulia began to cry there would be no end to her wailing. Even the Changs upstairs became concerned. Mrs Chang came downstairs and knocked on the door. 'Petulia, you mustn't cry anymore,' she pleaded. 'If you cry during the post-confinement month, you will go blind.'

'I don't care if I cry myself blind,' sobbed Petulia. 'Then I won't have to look at his face anymore.' Mrs Chang's words, however, did have an effect, and Petulia stopped crying. After a while, Petulia slowly clambered out of bed, threw on a housecoat and ventured into the kitchen. She fried up several dishes and piled the bowls up in a cabinet, intending to keep them to eat at her leisure.

During this period Mr P'u always frowned when he came home, and constantly moaned and groaned in despair. One night, when baby Griever disrupted his sleep, Mr P'u suddenly turned around and slapped his son on the bottom. 'You're insane,' Petulia screamed. 'He's just tiny. How could you treat him so viciously!'

Mr P'u stretched his arm out and looked at his palm. 'I'm a mess. I can't take any more.'

Petulia moved close beside Mr P'u and grabbed his hand. 'Do it again! Hit me, too! You can beat the two of us to death and then you'll feel much better!'

Mr P'u withdrew his hand and suddenly began to slap his own face. 'I deserve to die,' said Mr P'u hoarsely. 'I should slap myself.'

The next day when Mr P'u returned home from work, his expression was most unusual. He pulled a thick wad of banknotes out of his pocket and tossed it down in front of Petulia. 'Didn't you complain I'm useless and don't know how to make big money? Well, now we have a lot of money. Go and spend it as you please.'

'Where did you get all this money,' asked Petulia warily, as she stared at the pile of banknotes.

'Don't you concern yourself with that,' replied Mr P'u impatiently. 'I have my means.'

With money in hand, Mr P'u and Petulia enjoyed a pleasant week of extravagance. Holding little Griever in her arms, Petulia shopped to her heart's content. After she ordered a set of bespoke gold jewellery at the famous Heng-fu Jewellery Co., Petulia became much more agreeable, and her previous tender and loving attitude to Mr P'u was fully restored.

But one night, when the sky was completely dark and there was no sign of Mr P'u, two of his colleagues from the electric company knocked on the door.

'Mr P'u has encountered some difficulties,' they said to Petulia. 'May we trouble you to accompany us.'

Panic-stricken, Petulia looked at the visitors and realised something was very wrong. She asked Mrs Chang upstairs to take care of little Griever, haphazardly threw on an overcoat, and went out with the visitors.

As they walked, Mr P'u's colleagues told her bluntly,

'Mr P'u has embezzled company funds. The amount is so enormous it's incredible.'

Petulia was struck dumb. All she could manage was to hold the collar of her coat tightly to protect herself from the bone-chilling winter wind on the street.

'Mr P'u was accustomed to living the life of a playboy,' said the men from the electric company. 'He was used to spending money, and was unable to adapt to the changes in the New Society.'

Petulia then began to sob. 'I ruined him,' she whimpered. 'It was all because of me.'

Mr P'u was sitting in a tiny room in the detention centre. When he saw Petulia his lips began to tremble but did not speak. Mr P'u looked a sickly pale and his dishevelled hair fell in an unruly mess on his forehead. Petulia walked over, embraced his head and sobbed as she ran her fingers through his hair.

'I never imagined it would come to this,' said Mr P'u. 'I never imagined our life as husband and wife would be so short. It would appear that I shall not be able to return home. How will you ever be able to survive looking after Griever alone?' Finally, he said, 'When Griever grows up, don't let him fool around with women; men like me only come to a tragic end.'

Mr P'u stood up. He held Petulia's waist tightly and kissed her hair, her eyes, and her lips. Mr P'u's lips were icy cold, and a lost look radiated from his vacant eyes.

Petulia would never forget the last kiss Mr P'u gave her, a long and passionate kiss, almost suffocating her. For a long time afterwards, whenever Petulia thought about her last meeting with Mr P'u, her whole body would tremble violently. This tempestuous marriage was, after all, nothing but a nightmare, and Petulia often awoke in the middle of the night screaming.

*

The prostitutes of the Emerald Cloud Lane of former days all knew Mr P'u well. One day in March 1954, they met at the old cemetery to see him off for the last time. Mr P'u was kneeling on the ground, with cotton rags stuffed in his mouth. He was not in prison attire, but instead was wearing his customary light grey suit.

When the shot was fired, Mr P'u's brains splattered on the ground in a bloody mess, and the prostitutes all shrieked. Then followed piteous wails of grief. 'It's Petulia's fault,' someone called out. 'Petulia killed him.'

Petulia did not go to the old cemetery. On the day of Mr P'u's execution, Petulia returned to work at her old job in the glass bottle-recycling factory, with little Griever strapped to her back. She sat expressionlessly amongst the female workers, as she washed an endless succession of bottles.

Around about ten in the morning, Griever suddenly

began to bawl. Petulia twitched and extended an arm to pat her son and calm him down. 'He's hungry, isn't he?' said a nearby woman. 'You'd better feed him.'

Petulia shook her head. 'No, that's not it,' she said. 'Mr P'u is gone. Poor old Mr P'u. He was a good man, and I ruined him.'

Autumn Grace did not go to the old cemetery, either. Later, the women who witnessed the execution gathered at Autumn Grace's house to recount details of Mr P'u's horrific death. Autumn Grace just listened but did not say anything.

Her husband, Feng the Fifth, attentively served tea to the female guests. 'Please come back later,' Autumn Grace said to her husband. 'Let me chat with my friends.' Feng the Fifth left the house, but Autumn Grace still said nothing. When the women had finished the pot of tea Autumn Grace stood up. 'You can leave too,' she said. 'He's dead, so what's the use of talking about all this. I want to be alone, I'm a mess.'

That evening rain splashed onto the leaves of the French plane tree outside Petulia's window. The two-storey building of the Changs' was like a solitary island in the ocean. Petulia held Griever in her arms as she moved about the room anxiously. Later, she indistinctly saw Autumn Grace's face through the rainwater streaking down the windowpane. Autumn Grace had an umbrella and was gently tapping on the window.

Tears streamed down Petulia's face as she opened the door. Autumn Grace stood in the doorway staring at Petulia. 'Why aren't you in mourning attire, Petulia?' she asked.

Head lowered, Petulia avoided Autumn Grace's eyes. 'I forgot,' Petulia stammered. 'I don't know about such things, and I'm all confused.'

Autumn Grace picked a white flower of mourning from her own head, walked over to Petulia and inserted the stem into Petulia's hair. 'I knew you'd forget,' said Autumn Grace. 'I bought one for you. The rain was heavy and it's wet.'

Petulia then collapsed in Autumn Grace's arms. 'I hate myself! I'm scared!' she wailed. 'It was me! I ruined him!'

'No one can do anything about it. Everything between a man and a woman is preordained, and so is death,' said Autumn Grace calmly. 'If your feelings for Mr P'u are real, then look after Griever. That's all you can do as a woman.'

Autumn Grace took baby Griever in her arms and did not let go until the infant was fast asleep. She then watched Petulia take off Griever's tiny clothes to change his diaper. 'You're fortunate,' Autumn Grace suddenly said. 'After all, you still have a chubby little boy.'

'I'm fed up,' retorted Petulia. 'If you want, take him.'

'Do you really mean it?' asked Autumn Grace. 'If you do, I will take him home. I'm desperate for a son.'

Petulia was momentarily startled. She raised her head to study Autumn Grace's face.

Autumn Grace turned away to look out the window as she continued. 'I saw a doctor last month. The doctor said I'm infertile. I won't be able to have children of my own.'

Petulia thought for a moment then said, 'That's not a bad thing. You'd suffer much less without having children.'

'You really are the "well-fed who doesn't know how the starving suffer,"' said Autumn Grace. 'The suffering of having your own child is nothing. I just can't reconcile with what the doctor told me. But I can't blame anyone else. It's all because of the sins I committed in the past.'

The two of them sat together, watching the rain drizzling outside the window. Their voices were drowned out by the pitter-patter of the rain.

'The rain is not going to stop. Please spend the night here with me,' said Petulia. 'I was scared, but now I'm not, because you're here.'

'I wouldn't have left, even if you didn't ask me to stay. I came here to be with you. We were like sisters, after all,' said Autumn Grace.

Petulia and Autumn Grace went to bed at midnight. They cuddled each other.

'The blanket still bears the smell of Mr P'u's hair wax,' sighed Autumn Grace.

Petulia was silent.

After a while in the darkness, Autumn Grace sighed again. 'Life really is strange.'

Then, all that was left was the sound of rain falling onto roofs of nearby houses and the plane tree outside the window.

*

Petulia lived as Mr P'u's widow for a year. Initially, she and baby Griever continued to live in the same place rented from Mr Chang, even though her income obviously was not enough to cover the rent and utility bills. She was always cagey about how she coped with these matters whenever her colleagues at the glass bottle-recycling factory asked her. Later, it was rumoured that Petulia was having an affair with Mr Chang, the *p'ing-t'an* musical performer living upstairs.

Soon after that, Petulia, carrying Griever, moved into the dormitory for female workers of the glass bottle-recycling factory. People said she had been forced to move out by Mrs Chang, and the scab on her forehead had resulted from an attack by Mrs Chang using a wooden gavel. The scab later turned into a permanent scar on Petulia's pretty face.

The next year, Petulia left the city to follow a man from the north. The man, who appeared to be in his 40s, was sturdily built and had dark skin. All the female workers at the factory knew him. They said the man went to the factory to acquire a kind of small dark green bottle. Who would have thought he'd also acquire Petulia.

In the evening before her departure, Petulia went to Autumn Grace's home, carrying baby Griever in one hand and a bundle in the other. Autumn Grace and Feng the Fifth were having dinner. Autumn Grace put down her chopsticks to greet the visitor as soon as she saw Petulia silently standing in the doorway holding the baby. But Petulia then knelt down on the floor.

'I'm leaving. I entrust this child to you.'

'Petulia, what are you talking about?' said Autumn Grace, rushing to the doorway to hold her.

'I vowed I wouldn't remarry and would just bring up Griever alone,' said Petulia. 'But I can't. I still want to marry someone.'

Autumn Grace pulled Petulia up from the floor. Petulia seemed withdrawn as if she was sleepwalking.

Autumn Grace took Griever and placed a passionate kiss on his cheek. She then turned to look at Petulia who sat down on a chair, still in a trance.

'I knew this day would come, sooner or later,' said Autumn Grace. 'I'll take the child.'

Petulia burst into tears. The bamboo chair beneath her squeaked in concert.

'Don't cry,' said Autumn Grace. 'You can rest assured

that I will treat him better than you could. Do you understand?'

'I understand everything, except myself.'

Only Autumn Grace went to the train station to see Petulia off. She had thought about bringing Griever with her, but changed her mind just before leaving home. All she took was a bag filled with fruit, preserved plums, and some other snacks.

Autumn Grace and Petulia had their sisterly talk for the last time on the railway station platform. Petulia blankly stared into the distance the whole time.

'What are you looking at?' asked Autumn Grace.

Petulia's pallid lips quivered. 'I'm looking for the archway of Emerald Cloud Lane, but I can't find it.'

'How can you possibly see the archway?' said Autumn Grace. 'It's too far away'.

Then the train pulled away, taking Petulia to the north to follow a man. That was in 1955.

In the early days after Petulia's departure, Autumn Grace received a few letters from her, penned by a professional letter writer. But eventually, they lost contact. Autumn Grace could not imagine what life would be like for Petulia in the north.

When Griever was old enough to read and write, Autumn Grace dug out Petulia's four letters from the bottom of a trunk, tied them together with a red string, then stuffed the bundle into the stove to incinerate it.

Griever's official name Feng Hsin-hua – meaning New China – was given by his primary school teacher.

Feng Hsin-hua grew up in the Feng family and had no idea about his background. No one had ever talked to him about the complicated events of the past.

When Feng Hsin-hua was eight years old, he discovered a tiny round tin box under a bed. It was red and green. The lid was decorated with a motif of pretty women and flowers. It took all his strength to open the lid. There was nothing inside, except a pleasant lingering aroma. He was intrigued by this little tin and rolled it back and forth on the floor until Autumn Grace spotted it.

Autumn Grace picked up the tin and locked it in a cabinet.

'Mom, what is it?' asked Feng Hsin-hua.

Autumn Grace turned around. Her face was filled with sorrow.

'It's a rouge tin. Not something for little boys to play with.'

Radish

Mo Yan

During China's collectivist era in the late 1950s, a rural work team responsible for building an important floodgate receives a strange new recruit: Hei-hai, a skinny, silent and almost feral boy. Assigned to assist the blacksmith at the worksite forge, Hei-hai proves superhumanly indifferent to pain and suffering and yet, eerily sensitive to the natural world. As the worksite succumbs to jealousy and strife, Hei-hai's eyes remain fixed on a world that only he can see, searching for wonders that only he understands. One day, he finds all that he has been seeking embodied in the most mundane and unexpected way: a radish.

Mo Yan is the pen name of Guan Moye, born in 1955 in Shandong province, China. He is the author of novels, novellas and hundreds of short stories, and is the winner of both, the 2012 Nobel Prize in Literature and the 2009 Newman Prize for Chinese Literature.

 www.penguin.com.au

Marrow Yan Lianke

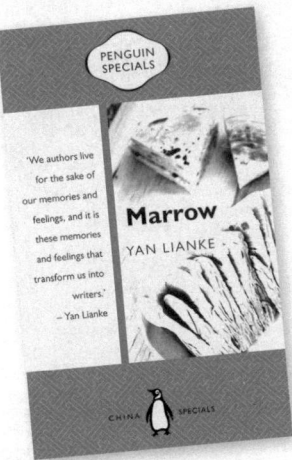

In a small village deep in the Balou Mountains, Fourth Wife You despairs of what the future holds for her four mentally-impaired children. A cure for the family curse appears, but it will extract a price so primal and complete that no one can be expected to make it except, perhaps, for a mother. A chilling and relentless tale of family responsibility and a mother's sacrifice, Marrow is Yan Lianke at his best.

Yan Lianke was born in 1958 in Henan Province, China. His writing oscillates between military themes and the Chinese countryside, the absurdly dark descriptions of which lend a surrealist setting to his works. He is the recipient of the 2014 Franz Kafka Prize.

www.penguin.com.au

Flock of Brown Birds

Ge Fei

In this avant-garde novella, a writer named Ge Fei retreats to the beautiful solitude of the Waterside to finish his novel, which is inspired by the Revelations of St. John. He perceives ominous and portentous signs in the natural landscape around him, particularly in a flock of brown birds that flies periodically past his window. The arrival of a mysterious woman named Qi magnifies his anxiety and sense of temporal disorientation, calling into question his grasp on reality.

Ge Fei is one of China's foremost writers of experimental fiction and currently serves as Professor of Literature at Tsinghua University in Beijing. Frequently referred to as the 'Chinese Borges', he is the winner of the 2014 Lu Xun Literary Prize for fiction and the 2015 Mao Dun Literary Prize.

 www.penguin.com.au